Proceedings of the Rabble

". . . I am so entirely satisfied with the whole present procedure of human things, that I have been some years preparing materials towards *A Panegyric upon the World;* to which I intended to add a second part, entitled, *A Modest Defence of the Proceedings of the Rabble in all Ages.*"

A Tale of a Tub

PROCEEDINGS of the RABBLE

MARK MIRSKY

THE BOBBS-MERRILL COMPANY, INC.

Indianapolis and New York

THE BOBBS-MERRILL COMPANY, INC.
A Subsidiary of Howard W. Sams & Co., Inc., Publishers
Indianapolis Kansas City New York

First Printing

Library of Congress Catalog Card Number 73-142480
Printed in the United States of America

to my mother
RUTH

one

Yes, everybody loves a parade. Don't you? All kinds, too.

Let me hear the cry of the horn, the shrill of the pipes, the bugles blaring, stirring the brass in my head! Ah, I could march off and murder millions. Small towns, cities, wherever the procession starts, there am I.

Even at its most ludicrous, in some God-forsaken village of our country as it comes by the dozen or so citizens gathered on the road, there is the distant echo of the great march, its terror.

Better still, on the thoroughfare of a metropolis, in the endless ranks that march into the distant blue, there is something you can almost taste, take between your teeth, it is so palpable. It is the very character of an era, a people, a city. In the faces straining forward or indifferent, the flags waved or slack, the sound of laughter, high jinks, razzing or disciplined cheering, one hears the decades coming on, one reads the entrails. . . .

It was a year of parades. It seemed as if there were a need for all the good, decent people of our United States to line up behind flags and go marching, marching through the thoroughfares of their towns and cities. Slogans, catchwords, maxims, words to live by were in continuous demand. Most of us felt neither to the right nor to the left on the issues, yet in the slumber of our lives, dozing along in the comforts of our prosperous country, there came the urgings of strange dreams. The world we read, heard about, saw on TV, was restless, chaotic, disturbed. Life had not changed for us on the friendly suburban block aside from traffic accidents, sickness, the report that the son of a neighbor's neighbor had died in one of those small wars we seem to be perpetually fighting; nothing touched us. And yet, tell the truth, in our dreams we longed to be part of that unrest, that uneasiness, which gripped the city slums, colleges.

It was undeniable that only one organization was putting on a parade worth being in, that strange unfathomable group, the Continentals. Suddenly their black uniforms seemed to be everywhere. On the surface there was nothing to really frighten you away: the usual potpourri of patriotic oratory and military paraphernalia. It wasn't hard to attend one of their scheduled meetings, salute the old red, white and blue (along with their black) and sign up to march. Still, there was something going on underneath. A kind of magic that had gone stale in the old organizations, the Masons, Kiwanis, Odd Fellows, Lions, something to really set you tingling between the legs; none of the hocus-pocus finger flipping and handshaking, but the real thing.

Know what I mean?

There were rumors. The newspapers didn't carry them. None of the wire services' stringers seemed to pick it up. Of course, they paid for a lot of advertising in the local press beforehand, slogans and such. It was always for a worthy cause. So as long as they kept to the small towns it was hushed up. Baseball Day in Minneapolis was the first time it got any attention. Then it was played down as a joke.

The Continentals were sponsoring the day, and they got the Minneapolis team to march in the parade. It was a festive event with big floats, a statue as big as a three-story building of the star —highest batting average in the league, a steel bat on his shoulder —riding just behind the players. Lots of bands, the city draped in the colors of the team, red, white and blue, and, of course, black. As an added attraction, the Continentals gave away thousands of free bats, autographed.

Just as the team marched by the reviewing stand, a bunch of hoodlums pressed forward past the police lines and began to whack playfully at the players with their bats. Furious, the baseball heroes who were parading with their own clubs tried to strike back. They started knocking into the crowd, hitting innocent people. The police churned in with their nightsticks. Everyone had a bat in his hands, and the players, panicking, had to run an angry gauntlet. One of the pitchers, a catcher, and three outfielders were brained within an inch of their lives and out of commission for the rest of the season. Worst, however, was that the statue of the star began to shake in the midst of the pushing. The bat!

A 30-foot section of sewer pipe—it broke loose, swung off the shoulder, round and smack—fell.

Scores were killed, maimed.

You can't stop something that's fun and part of the best in the tradition of this country just because of an accident. The whole thing made most people laugh. Minneapolis had been at the bottom of the league despite its star. Plenty of fans before the parade talked about trying to knock some spirit into the players. And there was a lot of excitement about the new parade the Continentals were organizing down in Atlanta. The theme was RACIAL HAPPINESS.

No one was sure what it meant, but everybody put his own interpretation on and applauded when monster signs rose up around the city with that slogan—white letters on a black background. You kept hearing it on the radio every ten minutes, just that simple statement. Reports were that the White Citizens Council and the Black Nationalists would both be marching. The moderates, too, were hoping the procession would do some good, because the atmosphere in the city was like tinder and an integrated event might throw water on everyone's inflamed feelings. It looked fine as it started down the main street; Negroes and whites both cheered on the sidelines.

Above the white sheets, newly starched, the deep wine red of the fez, the intricate gold filigree of African caps floated a Zeppelin with "RACIAL" painted on the silver sides glittering in ebony letters. The crowd was happy, watermelon juice streaming down sticky faces (free slices, compliments the Continentals), popping seeds good-naturedly into the files going by. From all over Georgia, Mississippi, Alabama, Florida, South Carolina folks had come. They mopped their brows in the July heat and gnawed on the soft pink flesh of the melons. Up at the front, where the first detachments of the parade were just about finished in their tramp down the official route and ready to break up, as Miss Georgia Peach, snow-skinned, a dash of brown freckle, waved, winsome, to the relieved mayor, a truck bearing a band of white musicians playing Dixieland stalled. It stopped so suddenly that the Association of Southern Sheriffs who were marching just behind the Untouched Daughters of Allah did not have time to call a halt and almost a hundred robust, overweight lawmen were thrust into the ranks of the fourteen-year-old colored girls. The sheriffs had been calling out to friends in the crowd almost an hour what they had in mind for the shapely behinds of the little gals in front. In the confusion of the shouting and milling someone . . . "Rape!" shouted a voice. "Rape!"

The crowd surged into the midst of the sheriffs, flashing razors. They overturned floats, musicians, tanks, the guns of the Army detachments lent by courtesy of the National Guard; even the riot helmets of the State Police disappeared among swarming necks, red and black. Overhead the Zeppelin burst into flames and rained down fire on the maddened crowd. Federal troops cleared the city finally, hours later. Over a hundred were found dead in the streets, some mutilated. At the very end of the route three bodies hung from a lamppost. Two were lynched. A black stripped to his underwear dangled at the end of a long rope knotted at his throat. In his mouth were crammed two white globes of flesh, tiny purple veins running through them like maturing chicken eggs. His partner, an obese white man, sunglasses cracked over his eyes, a sheriff's badge pinned through his cheek, had a mouth jammed with dark meat. Both were fitted with long conical caps, hollowed-out watermelon halves. Between them, upside down, screaming, swung in the nude Miss Georgia Peach.

Los Angeles, that lovely garden spot, a place of palms, fountains, etc. The parade had already been scheduled. There was some official remonstrance, but the important papers all supported the Continentals. America needed their patriotism. It was good for the country. No one else cared as much. Atlanta was going to blow anyhow. Maybe it was just as well it went on under the auspices of their organization. After all, the federal troops had been in place to move quickly. Atlanta was just blowing off steam. Why not?

And the theme was dear to the heart of every California politician. The Chambers of Commerce could support it 100 percent. Boy Scouts, Girl Scouts, Brownies, garden clubs, the 4-H, Young Republicans, everyone was out behind it.

HIGHWAY SAFETY

Just two words. They were painted on all the major roads leading into L.A.

Fluorescent, they shone out in the headlights of drivers. There were a few accidents, motorists who mistook them for important directions and slowed down, but in general people were on the alert in their cars as Highway Safety Day approached.

It was appropriate that a large section of the Los Angeles Freeway should be blocked off for the parade route.

Since it was just after the Rosebowl Cavalcade, lots of used floats were available, too. Full use was made of them, although in rather haphazard fashion as the large wire dummies of famous figures were simply thrown in heaps on the truck bodies, so many corpses, crude signs atop the pile reading "SAFETY."

In addition to the black ribbon pinned to the displays, special banners had been made, a bright arterial scarlet with just a pinstripe of blue and white. Most of the cloth bunting was oversize, however, and dragging behind the wagons; the colors were caught in the wheels, trampled under, clotted with grease, ripped into tatters.

The displays themselves were what counted. Hundreds of thousands of motorists parked their cars on side streets and concrete islands, streaming through the exits and entrances of the aerial freeway to gawk. As the floats crept along the freeway toward the parade route, almost a million cars slowed to watch the haunting procession, traffic jamming for miles in and out of the city, drivers putting their heads out. Massive sculptures of junk, hundreds of discarded, rusting car bodies thrown one on top of another; a flatcar of wooden coffins; 300 station wagons from the local town and country morgues, 500 ambulances, their sirens wailing; the entire membership of the Los Angeles and San Diego Campfire Girls walking behind these trucks with lowered heads; elegant black nostrils dragging the ground, troops of gorgeous horses from the Pasadena parade stepped in measured beat; a detachment of Hell's Angels who had been persuaded to dismount and push their jeweled motorcycles along the highway.

It was a sober spectacle to watch, keeping time to funeral music, somber and soft-sounding from the loudspeakers as it ground forward.

Communists, Fascists? Some idiot or fiend removed the "DO NOT ENTER" sign on one of the blocked freeway entrances.

Traffic that had been bypassing the parade route, speeding like hell to get out of the massive jam that would ensue as soon as it was over, poured through.

God!

The carnage was unbelievable. Girl Scouts, prize horses, spectators knocked down, run over. The Angels suffered the worst as they were passing right in front of the entrance pushing their heavy machinery on an uphill grade. Their bodies were mangled, crushed into engines and wheels. In the panic many were killed needlessly as they fought to get to their cars or, in them, started up and tried to drive away.

You might think events would be canceled after that. On the contrary, letters of congratulation came in a rush to the Continentals, the Chambers of Commerce, the city officials.

The Angels had been disposed of neatly. Despite the deaths, ambulances and morgue trucks were right on the scene. Finally, irrefutable, best display of a need for highway safety our nation had ever seen. As many were killed on the usual holiday weekend, driving. Here was a point to it all. A lesson.

L.A., Atlanta, Minneapolis? There is only one city in America, its filthy, indifferent blocks stretching for miles, claiming the satrapies of Brooklyn, the Bronx, Queens. If one were to move, to overwhelm those streets, who could resist the onslaught of the march?

The convention itself would be held across the water in New Jersey, the annual meeting of the Continentals, the first one, but it would be a sleazy sideshow unless they could first beat their drums down the length of Manhattan.

A long day is ahead. A March day, just after the vernal equinox, the bleak stretch of late winter. Black snow edges the streets and buildings. The midtown population hurried home last night, turning into the weather only to curse, bundled in warm coats, heavy scarves. On the Bowery, bums lie passive in doorways. Ice clots their breath. Those without liquor wait for the numb flush. Up and down the island blows a bitter wind.

And suddenly it melts.

The rank smell of warm air fills the streets. Naked, in brown and stony patches, the earth appears. The frost shattered, across the length of Manhattan, from gutters and backyards, a sweet breath rises out of uncovered trash.

It is a day for a parade. A real break for the Continentals. Lots of people would be out on the streets to watch. East Side, West Side, people just wanted something to happen, life was stirring again, you could feel it buckling up under your toes. New York wanted a good show.

It was going to be a special one. For more than one or two reasons.

William Star, his shadow fell across the sunny day. The Commander of the Continentals was not in the parade. He had not attended one of them. Star was rarely seen in public, anonymous behind his dark glasses. He was known to show up, unannounced, at small meetings. Suddenly the lights would dim, red candles were lit and in the flickering atmosphere he stepped out to say a few words to startled members. One heard differing reports of these appearances. He made an astonishing impression, but the purport of his speech was hard to make out. His men were mesmerized. They could remember a few phrases, "sacred finger," "holy country," "up yours," sometimes only adjectives, "clean . . . obscene. . . ." Yet all maintained they had been deeply moved and sworn absolute loyalty to his principles.

What were these principles? One received only garbled answers: patriotism, hidden joys, inside dope. Something had happened, that was certain. You could see it in the gleam of these men's eyes. Some rite had been performed which words could not communicate. There was gossip, of course, but no solid, factual account. Things were going on. Several larger meetings had ended in hysteria. Those who had taken part kept mum.

Today, for the first time, Star would greet his men in public. Also, he would be seen on national TV. At the end of the parade route was Grand Central, where he would speak shortly as he debarked his train.

Tremendous anticipation. The Presidential elections were coming on and parties were eager for the Commander's support. One couldn't be sure of his ideology; either side might benefit. There were whispers Star himself might run. The candidates proposed did not rouse much enthusiasm. We wanted something new, exciting, another direction.

Imagination! That was the key word. And Star had it. His

organization gripped America. It had a genius for getting at simple things that would rouse one's blood, yet—seemed complex, hinting at the unfathomable, the unthinkable, yes. . . .

Its catchword for the day's march hit right at home. Fires had been breaking out in Manhattan, the other boroughs. Garbage strikes left filth everywhere. The extra air pollution, rising dust, had half of us coughing our lungs out. There was anger in the streets. Nowhere to focus, though. All the agencies gave you the same answer, "Working on it," "Takes time," "We're attacking the problem," "Patience."

A CLEAN CITY

There's an antiseptic cry. No one could quarrel with that. All right, no more talking. Let's go right to the head of the parade.

Adolescent!

It breathed that spirit. Just on the tip of Harlem, way up Lexington Avenue, it began, a small-town parade. You know the kind. Veterans riding in glossy new Buicks, Cadillacs, courtesy the local car lot, painted on the doors. Felt banners held up by two grim-looking ten-year-olds in minidresses and white cowboy boots. *The Mighty Fifth District.* A little girl of six or so in shiny green sequins out in front who struts shaking her behind and keeps dropping the baton she throws up in the air.

Corps after corps of parochial-school buglers, the brass pressed to their lips, cheeks bursting with pimples, St. Angela's, St. Aloysius, Methodist Hall, Puerto Rican Boys Benevolent Association, parents, parish, neighborhood, out to cheer. The sisters, fourteen and fifteen, too fat or gawky to have anything to do on Saturday night but to practice the trombone; flushing under the looks of the crowd, reddening kneecaps and thighs exposed by the flapping skirts.

And the glamour girls. The drum majorettes, out in front, wiggling madly, desperate, between smiles and tears, twisting their sticks, trying to make them behave.

Older groups, too. Spanish Caballeros of Manchester, New Hampshire; kilted pipers of the Black Watch, Oshkosh; National Chorus Champions from Marion, Ohio, in blue berets singing "Hot Time in the Old Town Tonight."

The funny old model T that rears on its hind wheels flapping its fenders.

The genuine article, they served up hot, fresh corn. And the swarms on the sidewalk ate it up. The parade twisted from Lexington over to Fifth Avenue as Central Park was passed. Now they were right in the heart of downtown New York, crossing on 57th Street, at lunchtime, multitudes on the street, laughing, applauding.

Look at that exhibit, look at it! Festooned in bunches and swaths of black shroud, a pyramid of garbage cans rode down Fifth Avenue. The crowd squealed and howled. The cans were full of garbage. You could smell it in the perfumed salons and air-conditioned offices. Twenty barges, each half a block long, drawn by teams of white mules, creaked over the asphalt bearing the heavy steel containers stacked in the shape of the New York skyline, the Empire State, the Chrysler building, Pan Am, CBS—up to the third and fourth stories of Fifth Avenue they passed. A drove of pigs rooted and grunted between each barge, snatching up garbage jarred from the cans.

Fifth Avenue loved it. Despite the stink, window after window was thrown open and secretaries stuck out their heads to hooray and clap. Down in the street executives waved their attaché cases, threw kisses to the pigs. Empty paper cups, crumpled envelopes, torn-up letters. Wastebaskets were emptied on the heads of the parade; Coke bottles, sandwiches, boxes of paper clips rained down. Lighthearted, the festival air of the stench caught on. The noise was deafening, everyone screaming, throwing anything that came to hand into the midst of the pigs, on top of the cans, at one another. The yelling rebounding louder and louder in the stone canyon, above everything the high-pitched shrieks of the secretaries.

Unfortunate, the sound, like a whistle, echoing over the tops of the garbage, piping out tiny claws, beady eyes, whiskers; long and slippery black bodies, brown, gray, white, slithered up from the fetid rubbish, the shrieking increasing now as they crept down the sides of the steel cannisters, a moss, a vegetation, a mottled fur.

The street was full of trash. The pigs could not keep up with it. Several had overstuffed themselves and their bloated bodies sagged, toppled over, would not rise despite the goading of the drovers.

Attracted by the smell, great birds had appeared in the sky. They hovered, soaring over the garbage, the bodies of the pigs, the human crowd.

Which—awed, horrified—turned, trying to claw a way through

one another to get away, tearing at each other's coats, shirts, bare chests; biting, gouging, flailing in all directions. Rats among them pushed into buildings, up elevators; floor after floor of firms thrown into consternation as these small creatures, their teeth glittering with typhoid, sharp with diphtheria, swollen from trash, limped in the press of the halls, climbed through mailbox slots, air shafts, seeking the source of the shrieking whistle. Below, men and women pushed back and forth, pigs now milling with them.

A fever seized upon bankers, lawyers, advertising men. Rather than fight off the rodents, they barricaded themselves behind desks, chairs, lamps, or fled shamelessly, seeking refuge in the human numbers who poured down into the avenue. The smartly dressed women cowered on top of desks and cabinets, clutching their skirts, trying to protect the shapely flesh from bites. Many could not stand watching the things crawling toward them and, bolting, hurled themselves from windowsills. In the street the mob was bottled between buildings. They surged, trying to overturn the barges. A few cans at the very top did shake loose and fall, crashing down, spilling out a mass of rot, stink, worms.

Yet over the dead bodies, the waste, despite the flapping of wide black wings before their shaggy ears and long nostrils, the white mules continued to pull the barges on, on. On they rumbled to Grand Central.

All that day he had lain in bed. Not touching himself. The sheets were gray, soft with coal splotches. Now it was singing in him, hallucinating. It began above the knees, streamed through his body, which lay inert, a dead weight, became dazzling clay, shaped and reshaped. Abstinence, the Divine Presence departs from the unchaste. This madness he could feel touching him, wondering if the gas was on and it was the light kiss before suffocation.

It was bubbling in him, as if the blood cells were bursting, as if the sperm were breaking their vessels, only he had not put a finger on his organ, limp between his legs. No, for days now he had stretched in the wilderness of the four walls, praying for the vision, the fit, its figure to come, answer the act of sacrifice. A slice of cake, hard as rock, was on the table, a dried berry shriveled to its top. A dusty tea cup by its side. A full bottle of Irish, untasted.

Now he felt the room break into panes of light, layers of it, refracting from the walls, ceiling.

And slowly he rose from his arms, legs, torso, hovering an inch, then another, above the form of O'Dougherty, separate: his creature, himself. He saw the body, the silver motes, his head, the plane of gray through the room reflected a mirror of double consciousness: the long, thin legs, mantled, the smooth, unwrinkled cheeks, firm flesh of chest and belly, nipples, buttocks, calf, muscled, thin hair at the temples, each detail, pathos. The posture of the adolescent dreaming his own body, only grown with man's hair, fatal grass, covering over sexless child's parts. A man, O'Dougherty felt the tears, tiny, oozing in his eyes. Not yet, not yet. Forty. He was not ready. He had not exhausted the dreams of thirteen, twelve.

Alone, you had to be alone.

Among the ice shadows of tall buildings, the cold years walking through their lonely arcades, talking to himself, he had populated these freezing, crowded alleys of New York with phantoms. He caught up with them, striding beside lovely long-legged girls, who turned, laughing, shy, to say yes when he asked them to come home or brought him to their apartments, which he carpeted deeply, spread thick sheepskins, on whose beds, clicking crystals of sleepy liquors, he climbed into arms on silken flesh and drifted further into other worlds. They flee from me, he murmured as they disappeared into real crowds, real talk, that sometimes did me seek, stalking with naked foot within my chamber, that sometimes he would have to be the hind, lying back on the hard, thin cot mattress, feeling his own legs grown long and lovely, female, opening his thighs to receive his own ecstasy.

Narcissus diving into himself in the motionless glass of the waters. Who can tell the dreamer from the dreamed?

Into years ago, the still hours of the morning, two-thirty, three, the house asleep, he paced the corridors, staggering under the double burden, the school's reputation, his father's, trying to keep the Greek, Latin, French distinct in his head, the meaningless words lulling him so that he woke in a daze, moving off the bed, dressing slowly, dreading school with a sick stomach, remembering that he had flunked, been caught at cheating, was going in only to hear the speech of expulsion, the fury of his father at the breakfast table, and only slowly, as he groped for the doorknob, exhausted by the short three hours of sleep, stumbling into the kitchen, his feet touching the chill floorboards, did he begin to walk out of these nightmares into dawn.

Perhaps it had begun there, the public school, 300 years old, boasting of the same boring grind which had ground away all ease in adolescence, turning him to dead texts, rote memories, a mechanical procession of abrasive tasks against which hour after hour he forced his head.

In the long walks to the trolley and home he marched through forced retreats, Caesar, Hannibal, grasping at dead details to resurrect a life for himself. The disasters on his tests translated into holocausts, strategic withdrawals, honorable catastrophe. The Long March, ἐντεῦθεν ἐξ-ελαύνει, began the voice stirring as he broke from the green, flaking doors of the bleak brick school, treading the parasangs home.

Only the root went deeper, into age seven, six, beyond, in the blood; the old man who sat in the family home refusing to believe there was any goodwill in the world to him, the grandfathers who had raised hopeless flags of revolt, going down dazed at the head of imaginary armies, victims of the practical English. Some bard had sung them into kings, their petty valleys, principalities. So the rottenness was there in the stock and now feeling the ripeness which is the soft touch of decay, he knew that he had lost his way in the story. In his head, his body, he could not tell.

The gas was on. It was leaking through a rusty spot on the pipe. Odorless, although there was something sweet in the air.

He drifted down to the body again and, wincing, felt a twisting from his knees into his chest again, gently drawing him, turning, carrying him up, he was in dread as the joy spread through him that he was passing, the brushing of those lips, no, no. He had to get up, sit forward, or it would bear him off; only, his leg would not obey, his arm, the torpor lay between his limbs and his consciousness. He strained without effect in the sluggish waters of light, trying to move his impulse to whatever in the body jerked at the commands, too far, too far. . . . The body dumb, the cry fluttered furious now, trying to find a way back in.

God, it's incredible. The wind lifting him. He tried to cling; he was being blown away. "Mother!" he cried. "Mother!" Moving through the lips in the bed, softly, forming words, his voice.

Forced his way into the sleeping limbs, his will reaching out, twining electric impulses to tendrils, nerves, drawing, magnetic, and groaning, O'Dougherty's skeleton lifted itself slightly on the cot.

The room moving still around him, the walls settling back into place, sheets rustling in his lap. The fume of slumber still in his nose.

He sensed her in the strong beat against his ribs. Her spirit gliding from the room. Guide me, he prayed. Guide me through this day, as he stumbled up, stepping forward in a strange happiness, feeling for the soft carpet under his feet, knowing that the breakfast table lay beyond the door, his mother, sisters, his father bringing a bag of rolls in tasting of the frosty street outside and only splinter by splinter did the bare floor resurrect in him the bleak, empty rooms of his New York apartment.

It was a deserted office suite, the large reception hall his bedroom. It was wainscoted, scratched-oak panels, a hedge black with soot running round the walls; above, the plaster was gray, cracking. Over his cot in a broken frame barely hanging to its nail, a fly-spotted print of a freighter under the cobweb of a shattered glass, rust running through the paper, hull peeling off in scraps.

Two tiny side offices served as closets, filled with cast-off clothes, boxes of moldering manila. An old desk was pushed into a windowless corner. There were stacks of paper everywhere, leaves of it underfoot. The wind had blown through the open window while he slept and scattered manuscript and pages from the dozen open cardboard boxes sitting here and there at random throughout the room.

All the paper of his endless typing, stacks of rejects, first draft, second draft, he couldn't bear to throw them away. Now the heaps were hopelessly mixed up, retirement policies slipped between pages of glowing prose about woolen goods, refrigeration information interrupted by insurance data. A half-finished novel seeded the clutter. White file cards with quotes and lines of poetry typed on them dotted a lake of manila. O'Dougherty bent down and picked one up.

. . . that fatal and perfidious Bark
Built in th' eclipse, and rigg'd with curses dark,

It was specked with yellow. He had typed it up in Cambridge 20 years ago.

The long shadow fell upon him, darkening, hopes of great men's sons, impossible visions; an adolescent, he had rubbed shoulders with boys who would control the economy, Department of State, write the books, edit the papers of the country. His diploma was lost somewhere in the trash across the floor. The pieces of his own promise were there, the jigsaw no more confused now than before. Who can read his own? He blinked at the square of light hissing at him from the wall.

For days now he had stared into that patch; voices came and

went. He floated in and out of pictures, making sense, no sense, hearing news, inventing it, breakfast show, soap opera, adventure serial, documentary, and hours of his own images.

They filled the whole room. So that he was turning his head among huge showings of black and white, long, stabbing vertical lines intercepted by horizontal ones, vast snows, sun spots.

Dizzy, he sat back on the cot. A long, low moan shuddered outside the window, shaking the panes. Again, vibrating through the wall so that the papers seemed to tremble. A ship's horn sounding in the air shaft. The harbor call forcing up an echo of dolor in the wells of lower Manhattan.

Out of the waters, the mist, the damp clay, the waves receding, leaving the shape of Adam. All around him indistinct, blurred, the wet cowl slipping away from mouth, eyes, forehead. The earth under him oozing the seas above, below, still streaming off. And in that half-light, years, centuries, aeons, the intuition while it was still possible, whether he was man, animal, fish, bacterium, some element suspended, that will to meet, to know himself, to pass into his own substance. O Eve!

The myth, out of his own rib, split off to come to him. Had he created the girl, too, appeared to him out of his own flesh, his need, in that moment of suspension in the dream? Energy bursting forth in the splitting of that atom, what heat would weld the two, one? Was that apocalypse, refusion?

Lying stuporous on the sheets dark with the fossil prints, anthracite of long pink stamens risen in the bed, the lush orchards of his orgasms, shades, shades, upon the linen, he had waited for another partner, felt the touch of it still ebbing in his limbs. If Adam had waited in the watery darkness not for the shadow of himself but passive, will-less, inert, what wonder might have come? No form, no limitation, might have forced himself back into that body, that boundaryless all, that whole, breaking up not into thousands, not millions, but, Shatter me! he cried, Shatter me!

So many pieces, this jigsaw.

I spoke to you before, paraded my voice, sober, decorous, a bit smug but friendly—a veritable Milton Eisenhower's.

Milton! The echo of your famous name intrigues me. So I ask the citizens to imagine a shade of you in your good gray homburg as the dummy out of which I will speak. We will dress you up, though, give you a swatch over the eye, a piratical gleam.

Half-blind, I have been watching O'Dougherty in his bedroom through a telescope.

Ooooooh nasty, eh?

Especially in a man of parts who fingers, as he peeps, the gold chain in his vest, old, worn-out dugs, patting a pompous spread of belly, a banker, the confidant of presidents and kings, engaged in monkey business, spying on masturbators.

Haaa . . . Haaaa. . . . Have you read that dyspeptic Dahlberg on man? "Myrrh and unguents and all the spices of Arabia Felix are not enough for him. Mortifications and crucifixions draw him greatly. Lucretius asserted that human beings derive unusual felicity from seeing people drown. Each one is relieved because he is not dying, but he also trembles with subtle joy at the sight of the pyre, seeing a man castrated, or witnessing violence."

Yes, I, behind my *Wall Street Journal,* am mixed up in this. Have to be.

Have you read the physician among the poets, Dr. Williams, his diagnosis? "All the pure products of America are crazy."

We Yankees have always had that streak in us, a zany flash on the surface, underneath as deep a vein as the mother lode, our towns glitter, New Haven, Providence, New Canaan, New Hope, Los Angeles, Phoenix, their names like lightning rods hoping to attract fire from Heaven. "I shall cast you into the outer darkness."

Yea, and that eminent Colonial, scientist, witch hunter, Cotton Mather, cries back, "Let us humbly speak it, it shall be *Profitable* for you to consider the *Light* which from the midst of this *Outer Darkness,* is now to be Darted over unto the other side of the *Atlantick Ocean.*"

Yes, it is a land of visions, and what dangers therein, Amos 5:18. "Woe unto you that desire the day of the Lord! to what end is it for you? the day of the Lord is darkness, and not light."

Darkness, its princes are our prophets. Why not multiply evil? The Day will not come until we have. The worse, the better. "Shall not the day of the Lord be darkness . . . and no brightness in it?"

But I am being gloomy. "Arise, awake, or be forever fallen." The words of my namesake, "Hail, horrors, hail infernal world, and thou profoundest Hell."

A rain of black dots! Poking his fingers, O'Dougherty stared into the blizzard for signs and portents. He twirled his thumbs. A thick black line undulated before him; in the dim, empty room, high above the city, it coiled and writhed.

A face solidified, its lines no longer wavering, grim, unsmiling. Mouth open, eyes closed, it stared out at O'Dougherty, an empty hole. He could not be sure; a fly was buzzing on the nose, but it might have been a stray blinking of the Horizontal.

The face retreated, inch by inch, as the camera backed away, farther and farther, until it was only the head of a corpse, a body with legs and arms outspread, sticks in a scanty uniform. The camera stopped and framed the cadaver in its dark clothes against the jungle foliage.

The picture enlarged. It included a tall Marine sergeant. A young man, his face spotted by blood or pimples, a microphone held by an unseen interviewer was thrust in his face. The sergeant's mouth worked up and down, whether chewing or talking O'Dougherty could not tell. For a few seconds he watched the voiceless jawing, then realized the sound was not on. Correcting it, the set boomed with heavy artillery. The sergeant's words, half-audible in the thunder.

". . . Operation Cleanup."

The questions, too far off mike, could not be heard.

"Our casualties . . . real light."

"An arm . . . fragment in his eye . . . caught it . . . got it up . . ."

"Just mop up."

The sergeant looked out at his audience. The corners of his mouth puckered. His eyes glistened like a comedian's. He pointed down to the dead Oriental. "Charlie there . . . mopped."

For a second his face froze deadpan. Then the mike in front of him started to shake. O'Dougherty turned away. He heard the pimples, blood, explode into laughter. He heard the hiccuping swallowed up in steady boom, boom.

In front of heavy curtains, a handsome, clean-shaven jaw swiveled. Leaning back, quipped, "You just heard from one of our broom pushers."

A disgusted noise in O'Dougherty's stomach. He stepped back, turning, and paced the rough planks in front of the set, kicking at the frayed edge of the Oriental. He dug his heel into the carpet. Where was the telegram? It would be too late. He wouldn't go without it.

Facing around to the set, he fingered the commentator. He reached in and grabbed the smug pucker in the smooth cheek. Squeezed it until he screamed. The knowing eyes crossed and swam in blood. He dragged the announcer from the glass into the room, kicked him about.

O'Dougherty advanced to the glass. But before the ironic expression, suddenly wavered, swaying.

Limp, he staggered back, sinking into a deep, squeaking chair.

"Oh, God! God!" he cried, eyes shut, drawing himself back into the overstuffed chair, his flanks sliding down over the plush worn to silk in the hole of its seat. A game! He was playing a game. Forty years old, he could not stop. Still dreaming. The garters on his legs cut, steel wire in his flesh. No telegram, please! No Odyssey. His shirt collar was choking him. Blood stung in the shaving cuts of his face. Disgust ebbed through him. Take off my clothes, sleep, hide for days, safe under a pile of blankets.

Who had started this evening? Me, Dora, William Star?

He had been born into a line of fools, his great-grandfather who played Antichrist, his grandfather, a Jesuit, and the idealistic sot who rotted alone in alcoholic cushions, "My father," he intoned, trying to bring up tears of self-pity. "Pray for us," he called out. "Now is the hour . . ." He rose to his own eyes, aging, thin, foolish, a hairy scarecrow in underwear, existing by sufferance, ready to run and flatter at a word. He was forty and had no job, children, home. The one prospect before him, one to which he had drugged all his senses, was ridiculous. His head rang. Falling forward, he tumbled out of the chair. His knees banged on the splintered floor, jarring through a threadbare rug. He rolled on his side and howled.

Dreams sang in his ears, taunting. His temples worked up and down, beating a cacophony. None of it true, no conspiracy, no plot, a mad girl, screaming and screaming, he rolled until his eyes, turning in their sockets, twisted all into the dark.

Spent, he lay on the floor.

"We're doing all right now. I want you to know that we are doing just fine. The important thing is to have faith and not get excited."

A dull, lackluster voice, touched with a Western twang, spoke to him. O'Dougherty realized that it was coming from the television set, recognizing it with surprise.

"You just have to stand up for what you believe in. Otherwise you are going to lose the respect of everyone else in the world. I think we've made that clear by taking the stand we have."

Turning onto his belly with a cramped breath, O'Dougherty pushed his elbows into the carpet and raised his chest a few inches off the floor. He stared into the face of the President.

Under the eyes, endless late nights, shadowed. Trying to smile, the Chief Executive only seemed bored. He went on listlessly calling the roll of his achievements, summoning the electorate back to sleep, nothing was going on that couldn't be taken care of.

How reasonable the voice sounded. It drawled with kindly monotony over the Administration position. Yet the face was drawn, the channels cut into it undeniably sullen.

O'Dougherty reached up and turned the sound off. He watched the face, now moving noiselessly through its grimaces. Despite the pancake makeup on the cheeks, a television close-up lens threw into relief the wrinkles that ran down them. As if the power had slipped away in the long nights of indecision, each one wearing the beds further. Listening, wincing, shifting his cud hard, one way, then the other.

It was an old face, weary; the wrinkles went nowhere. It had run out of solutions, even enthusiasm. Only the dogged determination to hang on to power still showed. There was a grim set to the jaws, a crafty light in the shadows under the eyes. And the bulk of the President itself, looming behind the mahogany desk, massive, threatening, like some old bull whose weight alone makes him dangerous.

O'Dougherty remembered articles hinting that the Chief Executive could not continue without the affection of his constituency. The ugliness washed away in the midst of wild applause, deafening admiration. He smiled, grew expansive and preached understanding to the nation. Now looking out, he barely concealed his disgust.

"Oh, Father," O'Dougherty saw the same hatred. The ideals gone bitter in the old man's stomach, the edge of reaction in his remarks. "Grow up! Exercise some discipline!" while the face before him steeped itself in suspicion, drunk on righteousness.

The taste of defeat that had come off the concrete walls of school basements in the last years of the political career, the senator embarrassed to read the meager tallies chalked up to his name, begging for votes on street corners, tugging at the sleeves of old acquaintances trying to get favors, and the false goodwill turned to him, Sure, sure, of course we will, said so glibly he went sick at the sound of it.

The President began to slip down on the television screen. The jaw appeared above the Chief Executive's severed head, mean and narrow, thrust forward.

O'Dougherty reached up to correct the sinking horizon. He brushed the sound dial.

". . . I just want the people of the world to know that the United States of America is not going to be shoved."

Slowly the granite face, its lines hardening, fissures of rock, stone determination, began to drift across the screen. It moved faster, split into 12 or 13 identical faces, pushed across the glass in dizzying distortion. "Stop," O'Dougherty said, his hand at the box. "No more."

The clean-shaven announcer leaned forward, smiling. "Although America is giving the big push today for world peace, you just heard the President state we would not be shoved."

O'Dougherty groaned, sinking on his belly.

The newscaster said solemnly, "Speaking of being shoved, crowds in Boston gathered in record numbers outside St Paul's Cathedral today to view the body of their cardinal."

O'Dougherty pushed himself up again. On all fours, he stared.

The cathedral, the iron pillars of the elevated across the street, a photograph of the cardinal, flashed on. Blood in his cheeks as he saw the long, horselike face, hooked nose, knotted lips, tough, Irish.

"You bastard!" He remembered his father's shout each time they passed the prelate's picture in the Boston store windows. An old woman had hit him for it once with an umbrella. John O'Dougherty, crimson, turned around and tried to slap her face. In front of Filene's, on the most crowded corner of Boston. A mob gathered immediately and only a cop stepping between had stopped a fist fight.

In the coffin that prince pursuing his family, a fury rising in his childhood with relentless, omniscient power. An omen! Hope began to beat, knocking in his chest. He shook on his knees. He would do it. The telegram!

Should he call home? No, the old man was too far gone, almost senile. And dead drunk by this time of day. It would never register. If it did, the shock might carry him off. He had lived for 30 years on the strength of curses.

The news would have reached him anyway. The streets around their house would be full of women in tears. The crook that drove a host of husbands from the boozing of Saturday night, flint-faced, onto the hard Sunday benches.

The hand of God! O'Dougherty began to mumble a rosary, broke off, amazed. Jesus! Power of suggestion. They were sounding them off over the television.

Another photograph of this cardinal, a few weeks before his death. The face was drawn and haggard. A crowd of stiff-faced mourners. They looked outraged, shock wide in their eyes. The cardinal was an institution, Roman Catholicism, the pope, he, synonymous. The crowd seethed and pushed with silent indignation.

At home the bell of the liquor store downstairs would be ringing through the evening. That respectable horde wandering in the smoke of peat-fired amber, in holy mysteries, the fiery host, through the maze of Latin and Puritan admonition, the cardinal, his horse face . . .

"Brrrring! Brrrrring!"

O'Dougherty jumped up. Someone at the door.

Joints creaking, he rushed across the room. A shadow darkened the frosted glass of the door. Clutching its porcelain handle, he

twisted and pulled. It refused to open. He had pulled the bolt before. Reaching down, he tugged at the iron shaft. It squeezed slowly to the left. The door flew open, hitting O'Dougherty in the eye. He danced in the doorway. Taking the hand away from his smarting face, he looked into the hall.

No one there. The landing was empty. Bending over the banister, staring down the endless stairwell, O'Dougherty could see nothing. Frozen to the scarred railing, he listened for the sound of footsteps. The splintered steps, their broken boards, would echo a cat's tread. Yet he heard nothing. Silence. . . .

Something creaked. O'Dougherty was ready to hurl himself down the stairs. He waited, tense, for the next sound. Nothing. Only the echo of the first, expiring in the dusty hallway.

Almost a minute he hung, motionless, over the banister. His eye stung. O'Dougherty felt the sharp throbs of a headache. He distinguished the buzz of the building's electric wires. There was no other noise. Bewildered, he moved away from the railing, hearing himself crashing in the silence. Noted that the skylight was beginning to darken above him. Late afternoon.

The door to his apartment was open. He walked back in and closed it after him.

A yellow envelope was stuck under the door. He reached down, snatching the edge. Sliding out, it ripped. O'Dougherty held half a telegram. Opening the door, the other half was in the hallway. Holding them up, the ragged edges seemed to match. Turning back into the apartment, he shut the door again.

Inserting nervous fingers, he pulled out the two sections of the telegram from the torn yellow halves. Without looking at the message, he walked to the chair, sat down.

". . . on top of another. Through the rows of shops, the fire spread with unbelievable speed. Despite the immediate arrival of almost a dozen engines, the holocaust leaped within half an hour through four city blocks, whipped by unusually high winds. The smoke alone . . ."

O'Dougherty looked at the pictures of buildings in flames. He felt his heart beating slowly, steadily, insistently in his chest. He had to look at it now. If they were going to attend the convention, he would have to start soon. He had to dress.

He was frightened.

And if not. If the whole thing tumbled down. What? It was sickening, ugly. Evil out of evil. His stomach was queasy.

". . . felled dozens of firemen. A number of merchants who were attempting to rescue stock from their stores also . . ."

His hands unsteady, he brought the two halves of the yellow paper up, checked the jigsaw pattern at the edges. He closed his eyes. He opened them. Four words. Pasted unevenly. They spelled:

THEY FIT. WE'LL BUY.

O'Dougherty began to breathe deeply. He held his hands rigid and tried to read the message again.

". . . suffocated."

His stomach turned over. Ashes fell in the room. It had begun. He would have to go on with it. On the screen before him a maelstrom erupted. He clutched the arms of the chair as the room began to spin, rocked, back and forth, eyes opening, closing. And he was staring into the eyes of a double.

Black disks of the Commander.

The image dissolved into thousands and thousands of eyes, black dots, spotting the glass. Slowly the lens of the television camera zoomed in and corrected its focus, moving over the crowd, picking out races at random.

". . . jammed so tight that our television crew on the floor of Grand Central is unable to function. You just saw his picture on the screen and we are hoping to get a shot of him as he greets the crowd at Gate Ten. They have set up a portable reviewing stand and we see several loudspeakers here in the station. I don't know what the railroad thinks of a rally here, but the police cannot control this one. Talk about crowds, this is the largest we have ever seen in New York City. The entrances to Grand Central are jammed and traffic is backed up right down to Fourteenth Street. Our microphones on the ground floor have been knocked over and swallowed up in this mob, but we are lowering a boom now, to try and give you some sense of the excitement here."

A long arm swung over the packed walls of Grand Central, over an ocean of black uniforms squeezed so tightly against one another that there was no rocking, no movement, as the camera followed the progress of the steel arm swinging across and down; the microphone at its end suddenly switched on, and the roar, overwhelming, inhuman noise of the whole multitude, echoed deafening decibels, ricocheting the dials crazily in the studio sound room; the stiffened cardboard of the speaker in O'Dougherty's wooden box cracked, a voice buzzing at the edges of the tear.

"Did you hear? Did you hear that crowd? We can hardly hear each other in the balcony. Frankly, I can't hear myself think—Al?"

The smooth chin screwed into a pucker, indented in shock. The lips moved, calling out to someone. There was no sound. Something had blown in the studio. The announcer was still holding his hands on his ears, the fingers almost touching on the crown of his head.

"What the . . ." As the sound came on, abruptly, the image snapped back to Grand Central. The television lens followed the sweep of the boom.

"We've got the sound adjusted now. And, Al—we're going to try and get that mike down into the crowd and get some reactions."

The delicate drill hovered over the still, black ranks, then sank into the midst of them. The camera zoomed in for a cute close-up of a midget in Continental costume with Texan trimmings. The tiny man waved an enormous Stetson in front of the camera, obscuring his face. The boom sailed back into the air.

The slim microphone, its steel glinting, moved slowly over the heads of the crowd, a baton leading, hypnotizing. They swayed watching its progress. The pitch of the crowd's roar rose, a higher, shriller note. People were screaming as the swaying which rocked through the blackness caught bodies here and there, crushing them in its vise, a face draining of blood, its lips wide open, voiceless, lost in the tumult of the whole, the desperate, wriggling body slipping slowly out of sight, dragged under the panic-stricken heels of the mob, treading faster and faster, in the fear of going down as the bulk shifted from wall to wall. The building itself seemed to teeter. The picture on the screen tilted, as the camera and crew in the balcony were caught, mesmerized.

O'Dougherty saw it. The world leaning, toppling, and at that moment arrested, held still, as out of the mob there rose, in the midst of it, on the elevator of a lift truck, the figure of the Commander.

His arm was upraised in the Continental salute. Even at this distance, with the sunglasses, O'Dougherty could see the uncanny resemblance. He wasn't making it up. The pain in his belly was a thrill of horror now. It was some fragment of himself out there, here, and that madman could go on to anything from this moment. The motion of that mass ready to tumble, stayed at that hand.

The screams died out. Only the television cables hummed in the silence. And the cameras, moving in, followed the motion of the slight hand down to the heart, then up into the air again. The microphone, suspended yards away, picked up the eerie, purring voice.

"I pledge."

The speaker boomed with an echo of thousands and thousands who rejoined in murmurous baritone, "I pledge."

The camera moved in, drawing closer and closer to the Commander at the same cocked angle.

"Allegiance . . ." The word rose, trembling, above the resonance of the pledge, still resounding.

"Allegiance . . ." a deep and dutiful thunder.

"To . . ."

"To . . ." came the bass.

And then there was silence.

Through the vast public hall, across the stone floor unbroken by pillar or column, from one end of the granite space shored with tens upon tens of thousands, not one voice, one whisper, would advance the pledge.

All America, O'Dougherty was dizzy, millions, looking on, thrilling.

The silence! The silence! Only gradually did he hear the buzz of the cables, the heavy breathing of the crowd, the amplifier in his own set. His hand gripped the frayed upholstery of the chair arm, tingling. The camera held still. The picture, paralyzed at the 45-degree angle. High on the lift truck, over the white moons of the mob, the single figure, the Commander, his hand up, and in the snow beads of the picture, an illusion that sparkled in the distance, the one upraised finger, the third from the thumb.

"The United States of America!!!" The shout seemed to come from nowhere, but the crowd swallowed it up eagerly and barked it back, pell-mell, half beginning too soon, half too late, all that came over the set was a garbled, deafening noise. O'Dougherty was not sure that the Commander had pronounced the words, but as the sound of America died away, he heard the breathless, unmistakable voice announce:

"And to the country,"

"And to the country,"

"For which it stands,"

"For which it stands,"

The television cameras were zooming swiftly, not wanting to lose the climactic moment without a close-up of the Commander's face.

"One Nation."

"One Nation."

They caught the hand descending from its erect position in the air, elbow crooking in the black serge of the Continental uniform, palm closing in a fist except for the single outstretched finger in place against the heart.

"Under," the voice called, sensuous.

"Under," Grand Central answered.

"Un-der," it repeated, the timbre earthy, suggestive.

"Un-der," the train station responded, deep, throaty, gruff.

"Un-der," it asked. "Un-der? Un-der? Un-der?" repeated with a strange, passionate urgency. His head lifted back, his hand shaking on the black breast of the uniform.

"Un-der," moaned the mob, half-asking, half-begging.

The close-up lens slid in. Too far! Still tipped, the picture showed the bridge of the Commander's nose, his dark, thick glasses. For an instant they gaped, black holes in the screen, then faded into gray. The announcer materialized before O'Dougherty's eyes. The circles of the Commander's glasses still clung, a ghost, to the screen. Leaning back in his chair, the announcer stared at his lap, unaware of the image. The tip of his finger wriggled round and round in his nose.

"You're on!" someone shouted in the studio.

The announcer's hand slammed down on the desk. He snapped up into position with a ramrod spine.

"Under?" whispered the voice of the Commander. The circles darkened on the glass.

"The pledge," said the voice in the studio.

On the glass, the announcer looked right, left. Yes! His nose twitched, straight ahead, himself, in the studio television set, his own face and the ghost of the Commander's eyes, black and blacker.

"The pledge!"

A smile grimaced in patriotic dignity. Swelling his chest, he slowly raised a hand to the breast of his suit jacket. The palm touched the heart. He faded into deepening pits, the Commander's eyes.

William Star, Grand Commander of the United States Continentals, looked out at the country. The cameras backed away to get a full-length portrait of him, standing on the lift-truck platform against the enormous crowd.

And there, before America, his fist swung up from his chest. The single finger jabbed the air—"God!"

"O God! God!" O'Dougherty shouted as he ran toward the roaring set to embrace it and knocked it over. Eyes watering, he whooped and hollered, jigging around the blinking picture, waving the yellow pieces of his telegram at the prostrate screen.

"I shall rise again," he whispered, stepping off the lift. A Brink's truck was parked behind it, the armored weight immovable in the wedged mob. The riveted plate of the back door swung open and a hairy hand leaned out to grasp his arm. "I shall rise again," he whispered as he was jerked in.

"Beaudifal," growled the hand as it pushed him into his seat. Paul Gogarty looked at the Commander collapsing onto the narrow bench by Ark's shoulder. "Yah really fucked y'self in the ass."

Ark, the actor, smiled. He patted the Commander's knee. "So what?"

Paul Gogarty felt his jowls swell. The flesh came up bloody in his throat. His bellies ached. The belt was killin' him. Jesus, bitin' him. He wanned t'rip the strap outta his pants, beat the crap outta the whole bunch of 'em. The sweat streamed down his forehead. His bald spot was burnin'.

"So what?" Beaudifal.

He turned to the left, swallowing phlegm. Father Dole avoided his eye. In the cramped space the priest smiled anxiously, looked across at the actor, slunk down under the stiff guard of his clerical collar.

Dole was scared. He was crappin' in the seat of his pants. Excommunicated little mothah. Won't meet my eye, will yah? Keep lookin' fohr a cue, the actah. Keep it up, I'll stick a fingah in y'mouth. I'll grab that ugly little head of yahws and bash yah brains out on the wall. Dole. "Asshole! Asshole!"

Gogarty wanted to cry. His eyes misted. These bastards were daft. He was in fairyland. O help me, he prayed, Mary, Mothah o' God, ah'm a good Catholic boy.

There were tears in his eyes. He couldn't see straight. He wanted to get outta heah. He wanted to run. A few minutes ago they had the whole world in their hands. And peckah brain goes and gives it the fingah.

The seat of his pants was wet. Every hair twitched in his sacks, dipped in . . .

He wanted to strangle 'em. Sacred haht o' . . . What the fuck were they doin'?

He had thrown his New England Veterans League, the Knights of Vespuccia, the Nohth End Bookies, his brothah's political machine into the scramble. He had yoked with Dole's Daycent People's League outta Chicago, Ark's Western operation, Muscle Mac's Health Clubs, American Flag-Salutin' Society, Billy Jim Jones' White Southern Christian Caucus, and a host o' small fry. Under the banner of U.S. Continentals they mustered ovah ten million. They had a levah, a nut crackah on America's ballot.

If the niggahs played into their hands. If they could get the country between Commies and Jews. If the old general would throw his weight in, gettin' mohr senile every day. Lot o' congressmen, senatahs ready to jump. The cahdinal had been interested.

A big tear started in Gogarty's eye. Poor bastahd. He couldn't believe it. A beaudifal man, a haht o' gold. He'd got 'em outta half a dozen scrapes since the day the DA was ready to put his brothah and him away for election fraud. And the income-tax people, the old bird had really stuck his neck out. The tear, a long, salty drip, hotter than the beads of sweat through which it flowed, dropped from the corner of his eye to the side of his nose. Callin' them in, bawlin' them out, threatenin' the two of 'em. "Next time I'll let you Gogartys go to the lockup!" Gohd bless the old buzzahd. He just about took you ovah his knee. A real Irishman. And he had a good laugh, His Eminence, when they told him the Gogartys were gonna donate the income-tax cash to the cahdinal's Christmas fund. Jesus, the tears were joined by others now, drippin' down his nose, runnin' too, he almost fell off his throne with that. A real prince. A father. He had to stop cryin'. He wished he could call the old guy up now, get his advice.

His brow prickled. Somethin' was gettin' outta hand. It was like a religion or somethin'. It wasn't koshah.

In the dim, yellow light of the armored car's interior, a scum of white drooled out of Dole's lips. Bubbles dripped down the priest's chin, bursting silently on the silver edges of stubble.

The itch spread, edging up his crack. Paul twisted on the seat, the leather belt tearing into his flesh as he turned, a knout ripping in the bloated overlays. He was crawling with buggers. Scourged, bitten and stung. Holy Mary, Mother . . . "What's goin' on?"

Jones, across the tiny aisle, stared at the ceiling. The two fingers of the reverend's right hand scratched under his nose, snapping in and out.

I'm lookin' at you! I'm starin' at you. "You Protestant phoney! You pale-faced prick. You yak like crazy if they put a mike in front of yahw face. Don't give me the fingah. Yaaak! Yaak!"

Billy Jim Jones' watery blues were fixed on the steel ceiling, unwavering. Gogarty's breath come over them hot, heavy, moist. The red rims did not flicker.

"Mmmmmmmmm. . . ." It was Ark. Gogarty leaned within an inch of Billy Jim's chin.

"Don't spoil the party."

They were raggin' him. The skin lay mean, spare against the bone on Jones' face. The flesh stretched without a ripple, the expression impassive. "Kathleen Mavourneen," crooned Gogarty, "Awake from thy slumbaah." Nothing slacked on Jones' face.

Paul pushed his hams together on the bench. The itch was beginning again. He squeezed his buttocks trying to rub them against one another to wipe away the wriggling burn. The reverend's narrow string tie was under his nose. O Jesus, he'd like to pull that shoelace tight, knot it, jerk, Jones would burst into words. Gogarty gripped the bench.

Who could believe fish face across the way, fingahs stuck in his nose, had held thousands, a friendly voice goadin' on crowds gathered in small-town circus grounds and stadiums? Those long fingers now stationary in his nostrils guided the reins so skillfully that Paul himself had been driven forward in the press of supplicants, forgetting the decency of wafer and wine in his mouth as he tasted the spurting flood, dipped his hands in bloody . . .

"Shit . . ." Gogarty whispered, biting his tongue at the memory. The buggers were drowning him, crawling up under his armpits, into his ears, mouth. He rose in his seat, reaching for the reverend's lapels, shouting, "So what?"

The armored car jerked. Paul's head smashed into the ceiling. He staggered for a second. They jerked again. A second time his head cracked against the steel roof. He fell back into his seat, stunned.

No one said a word. Four figures sat frozen, one slumped. The vehicle moved an inch, then another, slowly, butting its way through the station.

His head was full o' red. Dole's face, Jim Jones', the actah's, sides of the cahr, the tiny window in the dohr. Two arms came up to his head. They were crimson. His head was ringin', buzzin', bangin'. "Stop! Stop!"

A fist battered on the bulletproof glass. The fingers were huge, hairy. A heavy ring banded one, a wart held the gold above the second joint. Opening the fist spread out in a palm.

The flesh was wrinkled, cracked with age, calloused like a workman's. It was the cahdinal's hand.

A hole in the center dripped bright red drops.

"You will deny me."

The voice came from inside.

Someone was sticking an icicle up his rear, bendin' him back rigid to the wall. A stocky arm, black with curls, swung up to his face, shivered in the air. His heart reeled. It tore muscle. "No! No!" he gasped. "Air! Air!" he clutched at the ceiling, passing out.

The air came slow, in small gasps, back into his chest. It was only a bad heartburn, the caseload of beer he had swallowed last night to pack down the porterhouse steaks. He had been warned by the doctors to cut down. Shit, maybe it was a stroke. He cautiously drew tiny breaths. The heart muscle was sore. He was scared. He didn't dare look at the window or scratch at the buggers. They were up to his scalp now. The slightest throb vibrated across his taut, raw heart. He sat still, feeling the in and out of each breath.

It was a sweatbox, his soft sacks boiling in a pool of salt water, floating on the bench, underwear soaked up to the elastic band—a yard of cloth wet as a dishrag. His forehead pouring.

The pounding had stopped. The armored car was inching along. He could feel it stop and start, almost in time with his heartbeat.

Mamma, he prayed. O Mamma, help me. "Let's get outta heah. Let's go," he begged. "I gotta see a doctah."

The bubble of gas pressing in his chest reversed itself, cracked loudly out under his hams.

Paul looked down. Shit. The Commander was crumpled in the corner. Suckin' his thumb. A puppet. Gotta jerk his ass to make him move. A whole fuckin' career was in that bag. The sweat congealed under him tacky; it was a nightmare whenever he woke up. As long as Star was speakin', it was all right. He scared the shit outta everyone. Fuckin' weird. He had seen it at a dozen meetin's, the way he got those fuckers cheerin'. Everyone at each other's throats, he stahted in, had 'em right between his fingahs, by the balls, dancin' a jig left and right, leadin'm. No one knew what the hell he was talkin' about. Sometimes it sounded like Jesus Christ, sometimes fuckin' Adolf Hitler. Like tonight, you didn't know whetha' he was salutin' the flag, shittin' all ova' it.

He'd taken all these dahlin's, most ignorant fucka's in America, had 'em marchin' up and down cheerin' to beat the band, gruntin', groanin', tearin' up the grass. He could get yah to do anythin'. Last night on the train . . .

Paul flushed. Awwwwwwww, f'get it, he told himself. F'get. I'm a sick man. I'm not supposed to get excited. His crotch stung again. It was a good thing he had put his fingahs in his ears for that fuckin' song this afternoon. Boy! Once the music stahted . . .

He wished he was back in St. Agnes' band. Happiest fuckin' days of his life, gettin' into the red uniform fittin' him so tight he was always afraid o' burstin' the seams, all that gilt trim and loop, white like an admiral's and the brass tuba biggah than a bathtub, the golden hohn, twistin' and turnin' around him like a snake.

He was the only kid with the wind fohr it. Liftin' it ova' his head, lettin' it down slowly like he was climbin' into the thing and when that low shudder began in its depths, it came outta both of them, lookin' into the mirror you could hahdly tell where the swellin' pink flesh and red twill melted into the blossom of round brass. Armistice Day, Columbus Day, Evacuation Day, marching along the main streets, deep in it, sun blinding on its stops, valves, oversized mouth, lost in the big thunder of the tuba, he drifted free of his fat, floated the whole band on the flood of his oomphah ooomphah.

Gogarty stared at the Commander. A sliver of Star's cheek glowed in the yellow light of the Brink's car. The banshee. He could squeeze tears outta rock. You wanted to burn the place down. It was like bein' in a herd o' bulls or buffalo. You stahted runnin' after that guy. You'd put yahw name to anythin', swear, pledge. Star put them on the road. Country was fohr the bihrds. Fuckin' imbeciles, only Star could get them goin'. He would win. Once he opened his mouth, no one could stop him.

All it took was a little ohganization. He'd called the newspapers, Paul Gogarty, give us a big play, TV, too. He let them know through the senator—he was on to their game. How the hell did they get their licenses? What about the full-page spreads every day from public utilities, the programs? They had hands in the pot. Shit all ova' the face. Get on the stick! Awr'll cram it up yaaw. . . .

The Continentals doubling, tripling, quadrupling, a one-hoss operation when he came in the pictchah, got them national press, arranged for Dole, Jones, to come in, had lines now to a dozen others who could really help, blacks, Mafia, Cubanos. Little more muscle, few more votes, some brass, ready to roll. The country in the bag.

What the hell was he gettin' nervous ova'? The crowd outside was hopped up. Ark and Billy Jim had kept cool. So Star gave 'em an enema. It was a good joke. Just as well the cahdinal wasn't around to see it. Everythin' was workin' out fohr the best. He began to hum, "Every cloud . . ."

"Silver!"

Star's arm shot out rigid, pointing to Dole.

Gogarty winked at Ark.

"A piece of silver!"

"I love the deah silvah that shines in her haih." Old Dole, always good fohr a laugh. Last night, afta' the thing, he stahted mumblin' worse than evah. He'd had a couple o' fits, they hadda throw water on him. Down on the floor, whimperin' and pantin'. Last few weeks he could hahdly make a telephone call. Whisperin' to himself all the time. Good thing his ohganization was brought in befoh he fell apaht.

The Daycent People's League, God bless 'em, in all the industrial cities o' the Midwest, Akron, Dayton, Cincinnati, Kansas City, Duluth, Dole whipped up chatahs. A big help in goin' national. They sent a brochure about the Continentals into every home that had bought a Daycent People's Bible, bound in *big* red morocco, all ——— pahts cut out and printed in an accompanyin' black leather volume, *keep outta the reach of kids*: or Daycent People's Index of Bad Books, a bimonthly publication, first class through the mails in a manila envelope with plot summaries of every – book published in the precedin' weeks, special features on the – classics. The Index had a subscription list o' four million. Membership was mostly in range o' Dole's lecture series. Gogarty had seen one of them just before the priest was brought into the Continentals. The little man, his lips pressed against the steel web of the microphone on the rostrum high above the crowd of rapt faces, high-school teachers, librarians, young married couples, insurance men. Dole's eyes large, his lips bubblin' over as the tiny red tongue flicked in and out, wettin' and rewettin' the lipstick there, his voice intonin' slowly with a careful pronounciation the scandolous passages he had discovered on the open shelves of their local library, neighborhood bookstore, the gravel whine pickin' out the worst delights, his hand caressed her milky thigh, stealin' upwards, she felt the ——— pressure, the priest sniffin' at each word, his tone cocked, outrage, suggestion, the audience strainin' forward, ears to the least whisper through the microphone, feelin' the stealin' hand, strokin' the thigh, creepin' upward into the ——— their faces reddenin', the breath comin' harder and harder in the auditorium and Gogarty himself feeling the stirring below, the stiffening, the throbbing against his truss as he waited, waited for the voice to inch higher and higher, pushing, pushing, milkiness giving way, up into the tenderness and again into the tenderness flowing with a honey that stung in his eyes as it dripped away in the still, still air.

Drops stood out on Dole's face. The carmine on his cheeks was sticky. Underneath the cosmetic, the priest's face drained. He was shaking as he stared, his tongue out, caught between his teeth, curling.

"Silver!" The finger extended from the clenched fist sprang open, a palm.

The priest lurched out of his seat. He fell to the floor. He crawled by Gogarty's knees on tiny wrists to Star's foot. He paused, eyes flickering up, then bent down to the black leather. The spittle ran over the shoelaces.

Ark began to laugh. A tiny smirk snagged for a second on the corner of Jones' mouth. Gogarty joined in with them. Jesus, look.

Dole stared up at Star, his hands crushed in prayer. His tongue was trying to push a word out through bitten lips.

The female hand of the priest fluttered to Star's knee. The white crew cut bobbed in the air. "Please," begged Dole. "It wasn't . . ."

Ark lunged forward. His right hand clapped across the priest's mouth, the left thrust in behind the clerical collar and snapped it back. He swung the little man away from Star, lifting him up in the air. The saliva streamed through the actor's tanned fingers. Dole's yellow eyes wiggled in his head, winking through wet drops as he jerked in the air. His face purpled. His eyes bulged. The tip of his tongue wriggled through under Ark's index finger.

A scream began. It screeched in Gogarty's chest. It scraped like a knife.

"Don't!" It was Star. Hunched in the corner, the Commander was climbing the wall. The noise almost drowned out the sound of Dole gagging. Between Ark's thumb and forefinger the priest's nostrils were pinched together. Doubled in pain, Gogarty reached out to pull the actor's hand away. "Hey, too rough!"

Two fingers leaped across the aisle. Jones jabbed up under Gogarty's throat, a prong, twisting into the flesh, squeezing his Adam's apple. The pounding began again, everywhere, head, chest, walls. All over the buggers were biting.

He was dizzy. The armored car tilted. Gogarty felt himself rising in the air. They were going over sideways. The tipping box added its weight to the blow he struck Jones in the face as the latter fell away from him. He collided with Dole and Ark, the actor giving up his grip on the priest in an effort to right himself in the toppling space. It only brought Ark into the arms of Jones, as Dole, striking wildly out, gasping, clawed their cheeks.

"What's the joke?" panted Gogarty.

Ark was laughing again. "Upside down!" he shouted as the car teetered on the edge of its wheels.

"Yah crazy?" A black shape loomed over Gogarty. The buggers swarmed off into a bat. It came down suddenly, sinking its teeth into his neck. Gogarty took up the noise that had stopped an instant before. He laughed and laughed until the crash collided with his heart and he swooned into the darkness.

One foot off the ground, Daniel O'Dougherty stood by his open window. The tops of skyscrapers loomed about as he pulled on his pants. To his right, through the battlements of two huge office buildings, he could see tossing blue waves. The Hudson met the sea.

Blue, gray, green, the sight of the ocean or its channel had brought him to the top of the dilapidated old office building where he had made his bed for 20 years now. He climbed 17 flights to his rooms, twice a day at least. It keeps me young, he thought, aging further and further in his hopes.

Forty now and foolish. His years stabbed him in the heart.

"Dapper Dan," he said aloud, with a look over his shoulder. A handsome profile, spotted, streaked, flashed above the dresser in the mirror. His flaking image bowed to him across the room, smiling, shirt tails out, pants half on, unbuttoned fly, suspenders hanging down. Since he left Harvard he had not heard that nickname. Two or three friends used to tease him in the dormitory for his elaborate toilette, the elegant clothes he spread out on the bed. The last of the cash had bought those suits, paid his tuition. His father's last grand gesture—Harvard and its trimmings. A nickname.

One-legged, tugging at his pants, O'Dougherty swung around to the window again. Hurry, hurry, hurry! Yet the blue patch drew him, that ocean, that blue stretching out under his eyes from the dormer window of the mansion, his grandfather holding him in a warm lap, telling stories as they huddled in the cozy attic before the view of Boston Bay. High on the hill, the sea below washed their feet. From the top of his dusty, forgotten building, he flew with the moving waters. O poison, thought O'Dougherty, kings and queens poured in my ear. Where are your shades tonight? Family ghosts thronged the room. The waters stirred. Over them he had seen the bark fleeing Ireland. The ocean curling gray with wizards, other stories fell confused into the tale told over and over, the sea turning wilder and wilder each time, the wooden chip plunging, tossing toward Boston. He lay there once on the eve of a hurricane waiting for its sails to break out in the harbor, wrapped in a blanket ready to go aboard, to join his great-grandfather swearing at the prow. Murder, in the attic he had drunk the blood of English soldiers, landlords, marched with pitchfork, hoe, the army of black-bellied peasants burning, looting, overturning, overturning. . . . They, the O'Dochartaugh, had been kings, his grandfather said. One had raised the whole North for a slap in the face. And burned it, too, he added.

O'Dougherty laughed. They were burners, his family. Obstructors, destroyers. The telegram lay on the dresser. Spoilers. Bitter, they were bitter.

"He had a filthy mouth." His grandfather chuckled, knocking ashes from the pipe, in the old house, a lean brick flatiron, belted in green copper, making a narrow, respectable triangle of the corner at D Street. Across the broad avenue acres of shacks stretched down to the four points channel and up to the hill, the fortress of St. Peter, Paul and Mary's buttressing the Catholic stronghold, its stone spire rising above the low roofs. Out of the window, through a haze of lace, the sea that inundated Boston steamed from iron stove pipes, a flood of tar paper. Down there, in the coal smoke, his red-faced cousins swarmed. He, his father, his grandfather, an older, nobler clan. And he was fourth generation. "Went to see the archbishop the first day in Boston."

Cahir stood before the carved door of mahogany, scion of the chiefs of Inishowen, giving the brass knocker a hard rap.

"His Reverence is in the study."

"O'll wait for him," in all innocence, starting over the threshold.

"He's busy."

"Tell him . . ." O'Dougherty winced at the window, the sea, green as bile, oh, the comedown, the fall, crossing a wider gap than the Atlantic, "the O'Dougherty's here."

"The who?"

His grandfather with a certain relish repeating the title.

"The O'Dougherty."

A soft rustle of silken skirts. And a soft voice saying behind the door, "No work here, you must tell him. We're sorry." And again the rich sound of silk gowns and little footsteps dying away. The doorman smiling into Cahir's face.

O'Dougherty breathed. The air was warm, yet a touch of winter ice in it, the odor of the melting decay. From behind one of the skyscrapers a rusty prow poked. It slid into the view that his window commanded. An ancient freighter, flag unrecognizable, between the sky and the sea, its bottom barely scraping the blue waters. "If you ever go across the sea to Ire-land," O'Dougherty sang out dolefully, his heel fumbling in the pants leg.

"Who the hell am I?" his father cursed like a madman, breaking the bottles right and left, tumbling down shelves of Scotch, rye, cheap wines, expensive whiskeys seething on the floor as he screamed out loud enough for the neighborhood to hear. "Who? Who?"

"Nothing to do but go north." His grandfather leaned back in the comfortable stuffed chair by the grate of smoldering coals. His thin, blanched lips pursed at the pipe.

Not, thought the little boy, before a few foul words had exploded in the servant's face. And there was the blast 18 years later, splintering the windows, glass across the lawn, half the rooms on fire.

"The woods. Drunken, callous labor. Yet he got somethin' out of it. He came back to Boston, a scar runnin' from his left ear to his throat. An awful thing. And a pocket full o' money. *'Finis coronat opus.'* Foundin' a shebeen."

"A saloon, a bar, our Irish hero . . ." His father sitting in *his* father's seat, the same well-worn chair, though the fire in the grate now lay dead and cold; Daniel's father picking up the strands of the story, with the morose sarcasm that filled his voice when he broke the brooding silence which kept him for hours without words in that seat. Like one lady picking up another's crocheting with a defter stitch and darker colors.

". . . thousands from Tyrone, Donegal, Ulster pouring into

Boston. Then the ignorant and hungry of the South, tens of thousands, Cork, Kerry, Kildare flooding the streets, rising higher each year on the Yankee barricades. And him in the right business, too.

"Only it wasn't the money. He wanted them in there. The Hibernian Societies, the O'Connelites. He herded them into the back room." John O'Dougherty's face flushed. The glass in his hand sparkling, half-empty, its liquor tossing back and forth as he raised his hand.

"It was Young Ireland. Guns and bullets in the air. Our priest-ridden paper here full of socialist notions. Anarchy, dinnin' it into the heads of the immigrants. Every Mike and Pat ready to turn right around home with a bomb in his hand. Our great mother Church noddin' good-naturedly.

"My grandfather, Mr. O'Dougherty now, walking the lanes of Boston, a well-known man, the faithful smiling at him. Not only the ragged ones, the drunks and whores on the back of the hills, but those white collars rising stiff and proper into the middle class. 'The guns and drums and drums and guns, haroom, haroom,' goin' home in triumph."

His father laughed hoarsely, turning in the seat, dipping the neck of the whiskey decanter on the table by him, back to his glass, spilling it over the brim, spattering the rug as he jabbed his drink in the air. "A dreamer, like you. Livin' in fantasies of what was goin' to be. He couldn't see himself as a saloonkeeper. He was a king, a chieftain, a prince, or some noble thing. Look at me!" he said, loud, forensic, rising in his seat, florid, staring into his son's face.

"Look at me! What am I?"

They looked into each other's eyes.

"A friggin' drunk."

He raised his glass, the obscenity still ringing in the small living room. "And you? What are you? What are you doin'?"

"Nothin'," he answered himself, starting to cry, "nothin'," sinking back in his chair. "That's what we're come to, nothin'."

The rusty machinery of the freighter's foredeck passed between stone canyons. A doomed voyage, forewarned, forearmed.

"Only it wasn't his fault!" he shouted, wiping off his lips the film of the drink he had belted down. "The whole world turned upside down. Who the hell knew the revolution would go right down the drain. They shipped off the lot in Ireland to the penal colonies. Not a word from anyone. Except their own, snapping at their heels, growling. That friggin' Vatican, seein' the specter of the godless everywhere. Eighteen Forty-eight, it was a dirty word. An atheistic plot against 'morality, law and order,' bastards!"

He rose again, tears streaming down the enflamed face. "They crucified him. And they did the same to me. You cut out my heart! O God! O holy Jesus, this America, this farce. It's nothing but a convention of old lady pickpockets. It's twisted the goodness and truth out of us all.

"All the old sweetness and poetry, asleep on a paper-dollar pillow. This city of unnatural bastards. And we," the veins stood out, red pencil lines, as he shouted, "we're more blue-nosed than the snots on Beacon Hill.

"They turned on me!" He stared across to the shanty town, his face a fiery scribble. "The whole pack of hard-pussed bastards. Not a smile out of the least of them. So proper, so fine on the outside, each one grubbing in his little soul for his own good. Sending queers, crooks, smilin' boys to represent them in Congress, in the Commonwealth. Bitter laughter, all that's left of Ireland. And the Church, permittin' it, letting them, mired so deep in the joke, only a daily visit to the confession box would keep them sane. Or the bottle."

He reached for the decanter and poured from it into a shaking glass, over his fingers, shirt cuffs.

"Who's to blame? God knows, we had to, had to take the public payroll over, had to honeycomb the Commonwealth with relatives, make a joke out of its politics. You and me and a few Yankee aristocrats can talk of fair play, livin' off the profits, a generation or two out of the cold.

"It was this country, it was done to them, brutal, cynical, not just at the top but in the very root of it, in the people—laughing at anything that didn't stink of money.

"They pity me, out there in the streets, that I didn't steal. There's real pity for me in their eyes. And they're right."

He started from his seat, holding the decanter. "And the Church put their blessing on it. I won't forgive them. I won't forgive them. It's rotten!" he screamed. "The whole thing, full o'worms, crawlin' all over." He flung the hand-cut bottle, shattering it on the wall, a thousand sharp bits of glass, dripping whiskey.

And the blast that broke the archbishop's windows, the explosion of anger thwarted, a generation betrayed. The long stacks of the freighter poured out their gray fog. Cahir's life went up in the dust, the ruined chimneys of the mansion.

The telegram burned on the dresser, a clear yellow flame. He had to act, only how? The forces of decency arrayed themselves on both sides, grinning equally, obscene. The Pious Bureaucracy, the Insane Crusade. He tugged at his pants, the damned things were knotted at the end, he could not push his foot through.

"Perverse," his grandfather had said. "A spoiled priest. And he was such a bright boy. The joy of all the nuns at St. Catharine's. Always at the top of the class. For a while your father even toyed with the idea of goin' into the seminary."

Only they were all perverse, he thought, bending over trying to keep his balance on one leg and undo the knot. His grandfather, kind, silver-haired gentleman, selling the saloon, buying a liquor store. His trimmed nails and tidy way of dressing, soft-voiced, sibilant, the little gestures of his hands as he flicked dust off the tables or curled his finger round a coffee cup, the female presence that hovered in the overheated rooms, in the tasseled and overstuffed chairs of the parlor, the gleaming porcelain and tile of the kitchen.

"He should have been a Jesuit!" his father shouted. His mother whispered, desperately, trying to stifle the voice that was drunken with grief, and more, "Shhhhh . . . shhhh . . ."

"Why should I?" his father's voice boomed through the whole parlor, thronged with crush of black robes come to do homage to his grandfather, to wake him. "He must have supported a whole college of them here in South Boston."

John O'Dougherty was in the corner, surrounded by women, his wife and daughters. He had retreated there, refusing to greet the holy brothers and fathers who trooped in to pay their last respects, hovering over the sainted body of the departed, Mr. O'Dougherty, a man who had given happily over the years in large amounts to their causes and programs.

"He took an intellectual interest in the Church. A great gentleman, yer grandfather." It was a man, silver-haired like his grandfather, speaking. The old cleric was addressing him in lieu of John O'Dougherty. And Daniel knew, had known for more than a year, that a terrible argument must have come between his father and these men. He could hear it clearer than ever now in the muttering of the corner. His mother engaging in chatter, trying to distract his father's anger. He heard it in the cautious sweetness of the priests, asking his older sisters to convey their sympathy and deep sadness to the senator. Deep sadness in the depths of the grave. Deep sadness would seep like water at the bottom of a well around the body. Little eddies of sadness trickling over his grandfather's face. Decaying, causing the corpse to rot in the earth. And they called his father—the senator. Knowing that John O'Dougherty hated the title. Would not hear it to his face. It was making him angrier and angrier in the corner as he heard it on their lips.

A soft hand, a perfumed one, reached down to take his. It was the elderly priest's who had spoken of his grandfather's intellectual interest. "Come on, Daniel," he said. The boy had never seen him before this day and it was disturbing to hear the father speak his first name with familiar affection. "Come over to yer grandfather and say goodbye. He would want y'to."

And Daniel followed, the unquestioned obedience to the cloth he had learned at St. Catharine's making it effortless. And he looked down at the kindly insistence of the silvery father, down into the wooden coffin, polished and gleaming oak, down into the bed of pink flowers where the face of his grandfather stared up. The eyes were shut and the forehead was speckled with a faint white powder. The lips and cheeks had been rouged, the red grease caked like lipstick. It made him shiver and he felt the delicate arm of the priest round his shoulder, bending him down toward the smiling corpse, a whisper in his ear, "Kiss yer grandfather now. Kiss him goodbye." And the boy found his own lips on the cold flesh of his grandfather's, the lipstick faintly sweet, his stomach fainting.

"Give him the kiss of death!" John O'Dougherty shouted from the corner. "As you did me!"

The elderly priest who had bent over the body, looked up terrified.

"You brought it on yourself," a voice spoke back harshly from the crowd of black robes. "Your ugly atheistic pride."

"I thank my heavenly Father for it!" his father cried, shaking off the women, stepping out into the center of the room. "My pride!"

"Your mouth!" the voice snapped back. The crowd hushed and gave way as a small man, his nose sharp and hooked, pushed forward. "Over the warm body of your sainted father. Whining like a schoolboy. An ugly voice to disturb his peace." Facing John O'Dougherty now, the cleric, barely five feet, shook his finger. "Who do you raise your voice against?"

"Who?" his father said.

"Who raised you up? Who put you there? Who gave you office in the Commonwealth? Your laaa deee daaa? Your nose in the air?"

"Nose? Nose?" half-choking. "Receiver General for the Holy Roman Catholic Church! I put you and your ignorant crew on half the payrolls in the Commonwealth. I found a job for every drunk you scraped off East Broadway. Nose? Theft! You wanted theft!"

The little man's face darkened against his white collar. "You wished to kiss the Yankee arse."

"Ss . . . spread that filth!" stammered Daniel's father. The tears were coming, the crying he could not stop, awful. "O God, God, inscribe it in the missal. You want my heart, my bleeding heart upon your hands. Ask me to kiss, kiss my everlasting end. You're right." The tears coursed down his cheeks. "I should have stole. O God, why did you not let me take, let me be a hero to my people, let me be O'Dougherty, the high and holy crook of . . ."

"The high and holy fool!" barked the tiny cleric.

"Nose in the air! Don't forget. When they caught my colleagues with their hands stuck in the till, I blushed. 'Close ranks,' the cardinal told me. 'Behind the criminal?' 'Why, John . . .' "

"O'Dougherty," it was a tall, close-shaven priest, standing beside the tiny man. His voice rang through the room without a trace of ill temper. "You've much to thank the cardinal for. And your father, too. This is not the place, in front of your own, to banter. We came to do your father reverence. Respect our sadness, make an end. Your tongue has cost you far too much." The tall man looked hard at the corner where Daniel's sisters clustered. "We know you as you know us."

His father's face was bright, scarlet.

"Never mind, never mind . . ." his mother whispered. "Come into the kitchen for a cup of tea." And she drew her husband off by the arm, his handsome face flushed before the cold eye of the priest, turned away from the smooth cheek.

The elderly cleric with the white thatch of hair came up to Daniel again. "A terrific tongue yer father has," he whispered.

"But a darlin' man in his day. Oh, a credit to us all as the senator. He'd a heart of gold, whatever."

Gold, gold danced on the iron cranes of the freighter as the sun sank on the horizon, melting the river in the gilding of late afternoon, pouring through the bleak latticework of industrial skyline. A sign, a covenant, the heavens coming down in his lap. A gold leaf, the telegram, a golden opportunity, O'Dougherty punned.

His hands tore at the knot in the bottom of the trousers. Why now? Why, a day before it would be useless, a day before the convention. Star was going to announce. He would run for President. A convention that seemed like a joke two or three months ago was now sending shivers down the spine of both parties. The polls showed the Continentals gaining strength in every discontented borough and town. A candidacy once set in motion would be impossible to stop. And now, the fingerprints come.

He bent down lower, trying to keep his weight steady as a single foot delved in the twisted cloth. To exactly the people who were looking for it. How? How? The telegram, cryptic, told everything, and nothing, nothing.

The message had come. He ought to act. He ought to call. Immediately. He ought to run, hobbled, one-legged, down the 17 flights of stairs, fly open, shirt flapping, to the nearest phone and cash in, cash in.

Cash in. Yours is not to question why. Yours is but

Why Why?

"We'll buy! We'll buy!"

Dora? Dora? Grab it and let's go. They fit. They fit.

The presses had stopped. They were waiting, ready to roll, roll. They had promised him, Daniel O'Dougherty special to the

And the Sunday magazine too, his name, feature article by the man who dogged him down, who stopped it all, who

He should be at the typewriter now. It was simple, easy. He had written it a thousand times. He could dictate it on the way over.

Why? Why?

Something was missing. He couldn't write it until he knew. Something? Everything. Nothing made sense. He understood nothing. He was the mouth, the prophet, the stoolie.

It was his last chance. Call! Call! You only need the facts.

It was someone on the inside. It was a leak. He had tried everything, lawyers, private detectives, a California DA, you couldn't get it out of them. The organization around Star was perfect.

For a year now, since he had approached the editor with what he knew, he and the paper had twisted and turned to get hold of those prints without letting anyone on to the story.

And given up. Hopeless. Had watched the march steadily on, the information locked in the drawer more valuable every day, more frightening, more dangerous. Now, hours before he announced, before the campaign in which any scandal no matter how hideous would be drowned out as the invention of hysterical liberals, suddenly, out of nowhere.

They had sent him a telegram at the beginning of the week. Sit tight. Something about to break. He hadn't gone out for fear of missing a note. Six days later, a set of fingerprints, a verified set, arrives at that newspaper. A set that checks out the one he has left.

O Christ! Holy Christ! Something . . .

O'Dougherty leaned back to breathe, drawing his pants like reins, his foot in the air.

His stomach began to tumble. He was dazed. The light of the river blinding. One hand clutched at the windowsill.

The red hindquarters of the freighter glowed. The sun enflaming them. The stern seethed on the cold blue of the waters.

I want to go, to go, to go back with it. To sail back through the dream-spotted years, the yellow pages of manuscript, the scattered leaves of failed poems, stories, articles, hours of odd jobs, free lance of trade magazines, back through the broken furniture, the sagging mattress, discarded girl friends, cast-off seed, rotten meals, routines, regimens, lists, appointments—to where? To what moment? To what harbor?

To that dreadful calm after his grandfather's death? No one had visited them. The family had gone out only on Sundays to Peter, Paul and Mary's, a somber granite tomb. The oldest church in South Boston, it was only sparsely attended. His father, who had brought him each Sunday to a different church in the city, letting go of his small son's palm to shake hands on the steps with dozens of friends, now stayed home. Daniel went with his mother and five sisters to the cold vault of Peter, Paul and Mary's, sitting, uncomfortable under the steady looks of the rest of the worshipers, who stared hard at the tribe of O'Dougherty, kneeling penitent in a half-empty church.

And going home, hearing the taunts of a boy, no bigger than himself, behind him, shouting, "Judas O'Dougherty!" he remembered gratefully what his mother had told him. How the empty church had been filled for his sake. How the spoon of silver shone in his baby mouth. And in the cold air, the taunts of the boy no older than he ringing in his ears, Daniel imagined St. Peter, Paul and Mary's filling with parishioners. The tiny child swaddled in fine linen and silk rocked in its plump mother's arms. While the organ played deep, sonorous. The poor standing humbly at the back of the crowded church, making room for the wealthy and important of the city, who crowded into the prominent pews. The baby's father in the first row, and the governor on one side of him, the mayor on the other. Both men piously praising the little one. While behind them a whole college of elderly Jesuits, a solid black wall of holiness and dignity, nodded assent. And throughout the great vault of St. Peter, Paul and Mary's, there were gathered the chief men of Boston, all come to honor the wee child. And the cardinal himself, his Grace and Reverence, had come to hold the tiny baby up, to sprinkle water on its head and declare:

"Daniel Donnel O'Dougherty . . ." And when he spoke the name, they all quieted down in the church. "I baptize thee in the name of the Father . . ." The drops of heavy oil stuck to the fingers of his Grace. "And of the Son . . ." The baby was anointed. "And of the Holy Ghost . . ." and you could hear in the high spaces of the hall a faint beating of the air. The incense was sweeter than you could bear it. And the saints among the people turned to them. The bearded fathers spoke to those about them and gave them knowledge of the true word. And the light in the church grew misty and dark and holy. So you could hear the choir singing low and beautiful, a Christmas carol. And the child at the front, wrapped in fine linen, glowing with light like gleaming snow. Oh the church was dark and cold now, the stone walls frosty to the touch. And in the back, the poor people pressed forward to get a sight of the little baby. In rags and torn clothes, raw-boned with red cheeks and frostbitten noses, they crowded to adore the tiny, gleaming child.

Even the shepherd boys knelt before the Holy Infant. Those

who had taunted it when they first came. Filling the air with dirty words and throwing stones at its crib. Now, on their knees, with tears of sorrow and contrition, they begged him to forgive them. They were ashamed before the helpless little one and ground their knees into the stony ground to show their penitence.

Yet he, marvelous king, ruling even then, rocked in the arms of his mother, a shining white baby, he had nothing but love for them, even those who would hurt him. And the animals around him, feeling the rush of beauty from his tiny beating heart, lowed softly. The mighty stag which guarded him on the right tossing its powerful head and the fleecy ram whose curls his childish fingers played with, scraped the wooden crib with its great horns. Oh, blessed babe, a shining white joy, in the depths of the dark stable. Sheltered now, for a moment, in the cradle of its wonderful birth. Above it, a star burning radiance. What if the world outside was cold and unkind. Filled with things bitter and unknown. Cruel children and older people whose faces were seamed with anger and hatred. High in the sky, that star would be flaming always, leading one on with dreams of its promise.

And hurrying home, "Danny! For God's sake!" behind his mother and five sisters, in the gray December day, the young boy could see, invisible to all else, a pale white star, fleeing across the passionless lead sky.

O'Dougherty shouted suddenly, his voice high. The river was a chilling, empty blue. The sun had gone down. The freighter passed. His left foot slid through the pant leg. Down to earth. "Hurry up! Hurry up!"

"I shall rise again."

And the hand grabbed me. The broken nails bit into my arm. They love. They love me. The hand was dragging me away from the crowd. My head banged against the door. Blood came up in my nose. Taste it. Taste it.

The hand suddenly let go, pushing Star down into a seat.

My body. You hurt my body.

A treasure entrusted into their hands. Yet they bruised it. They defiled it. Dumb, they were dumb, as beasts of the field, as cattle, as an ox, as a cow. Moooooo, he intoned to himself. Mooooooooooo.

"So what?"

Gogarty was sitting down. His neck dewlap, one flap over another. His face puffed out, bloated. A flat red nose, a smear dripped fat. A rock of flesh.

Gogarty settled on the bench. His thighs swelled into haunches. They trembled under his pink skin. A ring dangled from the red snout.

The pig was watching him. He stared at the floor, down, down, until he felt the crafty eyes turn to the other beasts in the truck. He heard the breathing come slow, in snorts, steaming in the yellow light.

"Asshole! Asshole!"

Droves of swine assembled in his rooms, butting and tearing at one another, their teeth flashing, fat legs shaking with greed. Awaiting the shepherd who would lead them forth. Into green pastures, still waters.

His fingers touched the metal seat. The curved roll of its edge rubbed under his finger like a gun barrel. The floor was metal, too. An unpadded cell. He stared at his shoes, a lace was loose. No laces at that place. Knot one into another, hang. Whose shoe latchet I am not worth. Ark had loafers. Billy Jim's were a preacher's plain black. Dole wore cracked old ladies' shoes. Gogarty had tassels, a fancy band across the toe, saw-toothed. His cuff was dripping wet. Tiny beads stood out on his forehead. The face gleamed. He blinked, trying to see through the mist in his eyes. Sweat seeped out of the pink dewlaps, dripping, soaking the cloth of the collar. Water spread across his belly in a dark stain. On the black shirt it hung from his armpits. The heat rose from him as he shifted his weight back and forth on the bench leaving damp spots. The air dense, a steam, its odor stale. He twisted, stinging with salt; blotches broke out on his cheeks. Send us into the swine that we may enter

A plague of insects, creeping things, a host of gnats crept up his pale legs into the moist crotch. Lines showed on the pig's forehead. A hand dropped down. The hand, hoof, barely brushed the lump as the vermin went back, forth, burrowing, crossing, recrossing. It came down again, smacking against the soft globes, his finger ends digging into the damp through the cloth, raking it. Insects climbing up on the backs of the dead, crawling faster, dying, going round and round in . . . And if the eye offend thee, pluck it out. Eat him! Eat him! Bite, bite, chew it up. Hunks, hunks, grind it, grind. The limb . . . bite it off, off!

Gogarty's eyes were wide. A sledge hammer came down again and again. He pounded in his squirming lap. His short legs banged on the floor.

The others were watching, the rat, the vulture, the mule. They stared at the steel walls, pretending not to see. As they tasted the maggot-ripe skin between their teeth. The swine rose halfway in his seat, his neck in rash, his ears.

"So what?"

His hooves struck the breast of the vulture. The bird was rigid. His talon trembled. The truck lurched.

Gogarty staggered.

The pig must lie down with the vulture, the rat with the mule.

For I will come with signs and wonders. I will be known by

Gogarty dazed, swayed.

. . . beasts of the field and the unclean animal. You shall love one another. There is no sin, except against . . . I sit among publicans and sinners.

The pig's head smashed the ceiling.

Blessed be the meek.

Gogarty toppled into his seat.

And the pounding began, the swine, the shitters, scraping their tusks, sharp with malice. Knocking louder, louder, restless, angry. They butted the truck, steady at first, then wilder. On all sides the pounding rang. The truck a drum. They had turned on him. Gogarty gave them the word. They knew!

They crowded to overturn the truck, squealing, rooting, ready to eat the litter.

Gogarty sat stunned on the bench. It couldn't be him.

Someone had told. He knew it.

Outside a crowd, animals, were hammering.

The rat hid below a white collar. The vulture stared at the sky with talons folded. A half-smiling mule, hind legs crossed, looked past him.

The arms reached in. The mob, human. They grabbed him, hands horny, scaled. He was passed down, shoved, dragged smiling, into the midst of cursing faces, twisting lips, noses. They yanked him limp and gentle through kicking, spitting; women reaching with long fingernails, filthy words, punching him. He gave his body to be flailed, ripped, pulled among a crazed assemblage, biting, falling on him. An ocean of crawling things.

Take me up, up! The rough wooden spur, scoring the flesh of his back, splintering in the skin, began to rise above the crowd, dizzy, as he felt his weight, stinging in his palms and feet.

Those pegs tearing in his grasp, and below, swaying, the mob.

The faces pushed together, distant. A frieze around the spar on which he hung.

Empty eyes staring, a boy bending down to a picnic pail, a woman settling on a stool. Some already bored. Now that the moment, the first one, was over, they leaned forward, faces set. Their feet had gone to sleep, their legs cramped. Dozing, they shared the dull pain.

The sun fell through the sky in the long afternoon, shadowing the bodies stiff below him. Ark? Ark?

Sunday morning faces stared up at him from hundreds, sober, regarding his torture. Where are my ministers? My anointed?

Far back in the crowd he saw the actor's handsome face. It stared back with yearning. In the depths of the gathering, Reverend Billy Jim stood with head bowed. Gogarty, eyes averted from the broken body, clutched at his chest.

"Let's get outta heah. . . ."

In the shadows of the canvas, red cheeks gleamed on a kneeling figure. A rat scurried across the cloth. It came to life—a whisper spreading through the Sunday worshipers.

They knew. They knew. Someone had told. Surprised, they pointed, tittering.

"Jerk his ass."

He tried to turn, turn away on the wooden beams from them, blushing through his mortified body, the pegs tearing veins in his hands, scarlet, he twisted his body on the cross, to shield his nakedness, hide his face, to wrench his buttocks round. The agony of his despair, the blood oozing in shattering drops, his legs, palms. God! O God!

"You . . ."

He sat, tense, taut, ready to snap, on the narrow bench. It was silent. No one pounded on the steel walls. All he could hear now was the steady echo of Gogarty's heart, thumping in the cabinet.

They didn't know!

Last night was a mistake. Ark had started it. And Gogarty joined in. Dole, too.

There were no records. Nothing. Everything destroyed.

Nothing had happened. He could call the . . .

No, they would come to him. Gogarty's heart was banging in his head, slow, painful, the tread of a sick beast.

Ark was wise. Dole was looking funny at him. The priest was going crazy.

Ark was strange, too.

They were frightened. Who shall ascend? My holy mountain. Who shall go up? My place. At my right hand.

Ark? Ark?

A mule, bulging with muscles, staring past him. His lips curled in that smile, famous, friendly, unnerving.

The smile.

Loops of neon, signs, wonders, wide boulevards, thousands drifting in miracles. In the crumpled magazines he read, lightning striking soda jerks, waitresses.

And behind the pitted counter he had lain in that hole, a rag in his hand, mute, mouthing the prophecy of his coming, his eyes crying out.

And Ark appeared. And saw. And knew.

Ark, who shone from the screen, cowboy, gangster, bishop, king, always moving in the same way, the mysterious smile appearing out of nowhere to the lonely, the outcast; Ark, whose chain of muscle and dance clubs reached out across the West to the lonely, the outcast, old ladies, young men, middle-aged, all who needed; preaching health, its baptism. Ark smiled, brought him forth. Knew him.

In the basement of the health club he met the small circle, initiates, beige belts, Ark had gathered. Their ceremonies, the gray-haired woman, laughing, slowly unbuttoning the top of her dress, dropping it on the waxed wooden floor. Stepping out on the mat, undoing the straps of her lingerie, so that she stood naked except for the stockings suspended from the thin ribbon of beige around her wrinkled belly. The young man stepping forward in his suit, dropping only his pants, then underwear—tiptoeing forward with his jacket, shirt and tie on, in stocking feet. The two meeting in the middle of the mat and beginning the mutual hold, arm in arm, thigh on thigh, as they surrendered to the exercise.

And later, the locker room, Ark and he discovered their kinship. Only Ark's was choice, his a sign, a mark, he had been branded.

It was games with Ark, play, acting. He was impotent, would bring forth nothing. Amusement.

Seedless, the mules were stubborn, perverse, treacherous, crossbreeds, domestic, doomed, one generation. His brothers.

. . . are born eunuchs, from their mother's womb, some are made eunuchs of men, and there be eunuchs which have made themselves eunuchs for the kingdom of

The armored car jolted. The claw quivered at the vulture's beak. At the back of the cabinet, something flashed in his eyes.

Lo, though I walk through the valley of . . . silver.

He stared hard. It was Dole's collar, the crisp, white linen gone gray, tarnished in the perspiration of the vault.

The priest looked up. His face bloodless, streaks of purple, crayon on ashen cheeks.

He had been blanched. The gray collar around his dead white neck, a mourner's band. He tried to smile.

Not Billy Jim. He had laughed it up, shaking his skirts. Gogarty, eyelashes blinking, had strutted in green sequins. Dole had cowered in the corner, afraid to flaunt the nun's habit, saying words to himself.

Last night, after the party . . .

But your will be done.

He turned his face, slowly, to the priest, his arm stretching along the beam, shaking, waiting. . . .

"Silver."

A rat stared up, its tiny eyes, its teeth.

"A piece of silver."

It grinned, the rat, watching. Another hand, the feet. Its eyes blinked back crimson drops. It squirmed in its collar. The last blow, his clenched fist, opened, shivered.

"Silver."

Dole fell on his knees. The priest was drooling. A string of beads bubbled over his chin.

Black, on all fours, it crept toward him. Its tongue out, curling, uncurling, dripping. He watched it inch to his foot. And crawling

He looked down. Dole's mouth was spread on the toe of his shoe. The black pump was shiny with saliva, a polished knob. The priest kissed it, again and again.

He heard the laughter, the guffaw of the mule. The vulture crowed.

A small bony hand lightly touched his knee. The nail of the forefinger brushed the inside of his thigh. A shiver went up. The priest looked at him, a blush, crab apple, spreading through the pale face. "Please," Dole said. "It wasn't . . ."

It was. It was.

He called for the cup. He called

In answer, the universe began to turn, over, over, over and over.

He flew upwards, teeth clenched in flesh.

". . . is it you Dora? Listen, Dora? Dora? Please, stop it. You're killing me. Stop it! Dora? Dora? I'm dying! Dora!"

Dora Horowitz, née Betty Bozoom, née Peggy Pectoral, née Madalyn Mammothlary, Babbs Boobies, Harriet Hopechest, Jane Jumbo, Katy Krammed, Beatrice Bangers, Bertha Bongoes, also Sally Snatch, Nancy Nooky, Catharine Ann Cooze, Sylvia Slit, etc., etc., slammed the telephone receiver back on its black cradle.

There were tears in her eyes. The phone calls were becoming more frequent. When she first returned, it was only once a month. Just to make sure—his sour hello, her mother's nagging Who is it? Who is it?—they were there, nothing had changed.

O'Dougherty, the fingerprints—it was twice a week, sometimes twice a day. That fire in the Bronx, the convention, she had called three times in the last hour. Her father had guessed about a month ago. Now he went crazy each time she called.

Why? What was happening? She was losing her grip.

Her forefinger went to the dial again and she began to draw up the first digit of the number, hearing it tick, tick, tick, in its circle, clockwise, tick, tick,

"Stop!" Dora jumped away from the phone with a scream. She was scared. She had to admit it. She began to pace the apartment, up and down her three tiny rooms. "I'll take a bath," she said out loud.

Not since three years ago, leaving Los Angeles, was she this scared. The bastards were on to her, she knew. She felt watched, trapped. They had killed that cop. She knew it now. It was no suicide. That story was dangerous and she knew it.

Why had she made the stop then?

Why had she gone back?

That prick O'Dougherty. Dora took hold of her blouse, began to unbutton it, fumbling, ripping buttons out of their holes. It was her fault. Why the hell had she started with this business?

Flies buzzing, the blood still drying, sticky on the white tile of the bathroom walls, flecking the mirror where it had spurted from the jugular. The drained face with a dark bruise where the head slammed against the tile. His torso slumped, pinned beneath the sink and toilet, a stained white shirt with police emblems and long naked legs caught in a red clot spreading out on the pink rubber floor squares.

Another clot, almost dry, surrounded the old-fashioned straight razor lying just under the sergeant's hand. Blood was crusted along the edge of the steel blade.

She did not like the look of it.

Dick Dong

Just as he had promised, on the kitchen table, a yellow manila envelope, the name boldly lettered, stood up on the pale pearl Formica top. The Venetian blinds were open and the bright, cold California sun was fierce across the green pastel walls.

Why? She had snatched it and run. Why hadn't she left the whole business behind, beat it? One hand clutching it under a trench coat, she hugged the folded envelope between her breasts. In the first phone booth, she bent down, holding it between her knees, slit the edge with a fingernail and pulled out the paper. The statement was signed as he had promised, although the signature seemed shaky. Only the fingerprints were missing. She had half a ticket. Half, and she fled.

With rumpled underwear, unwashed stockings, wrinkled dresses, she threw in a carbon copy of the story, a yellowing magazine, the signed statement, closed the trunk and fled.

She was sure, they were always making a buck blackmailing, bastard conglomeration of national scandal, crime atrocity, Hollywood dope, cheap crap they dealt in, someone at the magazine, at first.

Only as the bus churned (she had jumped it) eastward, she

realized that the murdered sergeant himself might have brought them down. His resignation would be noticed. Star would remember.

They rolled into the Sierra foothills, the peaks looming above them, the inner continent behind a maze of spires. Tall, silent forests, bare peaks, rock slides. No human sacrifice had sunk into the soil, made its outline dear, only skirmishes, a few Indians, outlaws, prospectors, a wagon train. You need a war, she thought. A little action. It was beginning, up there, in the mountain passes, on weekends, with stolen pistols, World War Two grenades, rebuilt machine guns. A line pledged to man the bulwark. Down on the plain they dream, the holocaust, neighbors lying in blood, wives raped, the children's throats cut. Old glory! Out of the furnace, men of the Sunset Strip Division retreat, hole up here. Each man's face burns with anger, holy. Ready to defend, to avenge, back against a peak, a part of these hills, rocks, trees, stone, hard, ice, brutal, stone.

Suicide? The sergeant was sunk in disgust. Their first appointment, his weather-beaten face creased by years on the force into a hard-bitten grimace, could barely look at her, as if it were his own story, a confession. His tanned-leather fingers beat a drum roll on the Formica tabletop, leaping again and again to a starched white collar, tugging at the shirt as if to give himself air.

He mumbled it, breaking off, starting again, sweating. It was the worst session she had ever gone through and she shoved her notebook under the nose of raped women, kidnap victims, parents of murdered children; took down the garbled ravings of maniacs, hysterics, schizophrenics. And he, a tough old buzzard, his beak stuck in the American backside for over two decades.

Dick Dong—he hadn't expected a woman. It startled him at the door. She was using male pseudonyms. He had picked her *nom de plume* out of the magazine, writing in to volunteer information. Under that last one, Dick Dong, she had been getting more vicious, brutal, too nasty even for the magazine. He had almost torn off his collar telling her.

The bus pumped up every last bit of monoxide and inched toward the high, bare ridges. For one moment, at a ramshackle diner where the passengers piled out to grab a cup of coffee and a bite, behind the door of the ladies' room, perched on the single specked white seat, she had trembled. The two bull-necked cops seated at the counter, the way they had eyed her, a lewd laugh of recognition, shouldering heavy beef chest through the door, snapping the fragile rusty hook, tearing off the underwear bunched around her ankles, one wrapping it around her throat, while the other, for kicks, took down his pants.

She froze, unable to move. Froze until the irritable honk of the bus outside woke her from the reverie.

The button at his throat had popped. From the Sierras the groaning chassis dropped down quickly into the desert, Dora's iron grip on the armrest gradually unbending. And mumbling, he began to pull at his shirt cuffs. Suicide, suicide, suicide, miles and miles of sand running through her thoughts, an endless hourglass, her terror sifting through it again and again until it seemed impossible.

America was too huge. The desert stretched into state after state. Somewhere in the reaches of these barrens it would spend itself. They would stumble, small, insignificant, the poison burning off. Sand blew in her hair, against her cheeks, nose, eyes. A blizzard engulfed the bus. They twisted and turned in a storm of it. Sand everywhere, blotting, blotting. She was free, free. Lost in the storm and she changed her direction.

Dora turned to the bathtub, cramped between her kitchen wall and sink, pulled the blouse out of her skirt, flung it on the floor. She reached behind her back, unsnapping the brassiere. Two large breasts slipped out of the halter. She bent down to the faucets, brushing them against the cold porcelain rim. The nubs stood up.

Water splashed below her in the tub. She leaned over farther, letting the heavy tits dip slowly, down, down.

Fire! The water was scalding, her arms came up to cradle the scalded nipples, shivering in the shock, thrown back from the tub, electricity.

Down the cast-iron stairs past the medieval apparatus, the tables for strapping patients on, the buckles, electrodes, for hands and feet, the discarded tubs of water therapy stacked against the cellar walls. She shivered.

The female attendant, a frowsy old woman, giggling to herself, former patient, motioned toward a locked door at the end of the cellar. Dora had the report in her hand. They had given it to her in the hospital office. She knew it by heart. The giggle began again. The attendant unlocked the door and put out a hand.

Dora flinched as the hard, curling nails grasped her, the old woman's fingertips, grotesque knobs thick as bone. Through the flesh hung in withered sacks, wrinkled around the knuckles, the nail thrust. Dora tugged, pulling her hand from the horny grasp. She looked into the open room. Snow fell through the air and caked as dust on cases and cases of files. She followed the other's hobbling gait down rows of cabinets. They stopped before a battered green one, its paint broken out in bubbles, flaking away to show the tin underneath. The old woman's lips began to twitch, the giggles a seizure, as she took a brass pin out of her apron and turned it in the cabinet's keyhole. The drawer slid out easily.

Ashes. It was full of ashes.

Dora winced. Her breasts hurt.

The steam of the scalding water filled the tiny room with mist, clouding windows and the wall mirror. She went to the cabinet over the bathtub and took out a jar of vaseline, smearing the jelly on her nipples. She bent down to turn off the hissing tap. The knob was almost too hot to touch.

His fingerprints were ashes.

O'Dougherty appeared out of a haze of sweet, thick smoke. A goat's face. She backed away from it, breaking off her stare abruptly, fleeing the handsome, pleading eyes, in the crowd at the party. He was following her. She watched him shove in the seedy group of pornography moviemakers, editors, promotion men, as she squirmed through, wriggling toward a tiny balcony. The glass doors, their panes patched with cardboard, opened outward and pushing, she slipped. . . .

The city fell away below her, stone canyons, blind air shafts, alleyways. Deep in their abyss, garbage cans, shattered glass. She gripped the shaky wooden rail of the balcony. It was hundreds of feet above the street.

"Hey!" O'Dougherty shouted through one of the holes in the door panes.

She didn't turn around but stared down into the alleys.

"Can I come out?"

After a minute of silence, he swung the doors open and took a step toward her.

"Hi!"

She felt the buds stiffen in her cotton cups. Between her legs the edge of her underwear rubbed. It tickled, tickled.

"My name is O'Dougherty."

In thousands of tiny points, she bristled, excited. Her skin rose, coruscating. . . .

"Daniel O'Dougherty."

The city below, its countless lights, broke in her eyes as if they were prisms, reflecting through her body, breaking into beams.

"What's yours?"

She could barely stand.

"What's yours?"

She would topple over, into the city.

"At least be polite."

Not looking behind, she whispered, "Drop dead."

"What?"

She turned to him, her voice shaking, saying softly, "Drop dead."

The current of tension passed through O'Dougherty. His face went white. "All right," he said in a low voice. He put one foot on the shaky wooden railing, hoisting himself up, "All right."

The banister swayed, then cracked. The scream at the table began, her mother reaching over to slap with one hand, the other fist banging on the top. Her father stood up on the chair, brandishing the knife, the dull butter knife.

He pushed the silver blade against his throat. "All right?" It was the end of a long argument. "You got to help out. You got to be in the store. I can't get a replacement. College is too much. We can't afford. Never mind a scholarship. Never mind three dollars somewhere else. I got to have you. Everyone helps out. It's a family. A family!

"A family!" he screamed, pressing the blade harder into his Adam's apple. "A Rabbi! I was . . . look at me, look what I gave up. I'm under socks, lingerie. For who? I'm in hiding. I knew everything? Your mother taught me. A store her father gave me, a mortgage, a year's credit. In the toilet I study. I wipe my ass and read Talmud. No more! No more! Everyone is free, free. No family! No family!"

He threw himself on the white tablecloth and snatched up the steak knife. The stainless steel shattered into electric beams.

"All right?"

He slowly pushed its point into his throat. The blood oozed up dark, venous. Mendel Horowitz tottered. Dora threw herself at his legs. "Don't, don't!" she screamed, the tears welling up. Blinded, she pulled him toward her, covering his face with kisses, clutching his arms, pressing him against her breasts, heaving, heaving, her lips pressing wet into his open mouth, biting his tongue.

The banister crashed far below, in an alley.

Dora reached to her hip, pulling the tag of her zipper. She yanked her short woolen skirt down a few inches, then peeled the panties off her rump. They fell about her ankles.

Hobbled, she took a few steps toward the bathtub. Bending over to turn the cold tap, the heat rose, scarlet, through her.

The deputy stood behind her.

His heavy twill trousers were hunched just above his kneecaps. The black leather boots held them there; a ruffle of white underwear on top of the police blue. His thighs were hairless.

She pulled at the doorknob. He had her bra in his hands. The skirt was tangled in her feet.

"Where yew goin'?" he asked, jocular.

She heard the cowboy boots behind her, shivering the floor. She tugged at the scratched brass doorknob, then pushed against it, ready to get out.

"We ain't had no soch'll inter-curse."

The cold brass brushed against her. Terrified, blushing, she climbed, pressed against the metal bulb.

"No," she whispered.

Flanks, trembling white flanks, mounted her backside. The animal's bulk bending her down, its stiff under muscle engorging her, wooden, its breath hot in her ears, its nostrils snorting on her neck.

She couldn't move. She felt the door spinning before her, the room turning. Her behind quivered with heat, burning, through her whole body. She bent lower, to open, lower.

"I'll be," crammed, she heard behind her between the battering creature's haunches, "a goddamn virgin."

The Greyhound had left her in Davenport. She transferred to a local line, a red and white bus that wheezed from one town to another, rolling, sluggish country, small farm after small farm, a few buildings cluttered here and there along the road and the bus would stop. Endless stopping, starting, mile, mile, until any quaintness wore away, the land, land, one jerked in boredom by the window, desperate for a book, a magazine. Dora didn't dare. Not miss. How far—the tight-lipped driver wouldn't answer.

"Don't worry, ma'am," he said the third time she asked. "You'll hear."

The names of one roadside stop after another, she listened to him, jarred awake from a semi-sleep by the bus's brakes. Some of the larger towns had a Woolworth's, a drugstore, an ice-cream parlor. Others, no more than a garage, diner, cement blockhouses in the middle of prairie farmland.

She had started it again. Why? O'Dougherty should have been the one to go. He had offered. They needed records. A set of fingerprints. Information. Why had she insisted? Refused to tell him the town. Set out on her own.

The bus jogged into the dusk.

The narrow country road stretching ahead seemed to lead nowhere. As if its reality had trailed off behind them. The repetition of the same farm houses and fields, before a dreary reminder of the uniform landscape, now eerie as the horizon sank into a slow gray darkness. Lights flickered here and there. The roadside swarmed with shadows. A pallid yellow stained the interior of the bus. The faces around her were forbidding. No smiles. The mouths of the men and women who got on tightened, thin lines, knots. She felt them watching, judging, a single girl in a fashionable dress, alone, luggage. As they stopped barely visible, a man came forward to the window in the rose glow thrown by the neon sign of a luncheonette. He was obese. She could not look away. Elephantine, he leaned against the window. Under a torn cowboy hat, its felt crown spotted, a pig's face. His eyes pink with lust streaked as the bus pulled away, lips blubbering on the glass.

Looking up, the driver's face met her in the mirror over his seat. He continued to stare, not watching the road as he drove.

The other passengers too, out of the corner of their eyes, breathing tense and heavy, over the engines of the bus.

And her breathing fell in with theirs, gripped, her chest rose and fell in the iron lung of their suppressed breath, hunger, curiosity, desire, they exhaled horror in the insane tedium of the Midwestern night.

Dreamed with the farmer in crumpled khaki work pants, his lean, sunburned face sucked in, of grinding the wife to hamburg, raising the axe as she leaned over the kitchen sink, to give her a hard blow with the back of it, just enough to stagger her, time to take careful aim as she wobbled and he hit her at the base of the spine, paralyzing; then a few knocks in the stomach to start the inside bleeding, dig the bones in, rib case, intestines, make sure there was plenty of circulation to give the flesh a nice bloody taste. Of course, there was too much for one meal. You had to hack it off in smaller pieces, an arm or leg joint, and the small soup goodies, nose and ears. Plenty of room in the freezer.

She was rolling around on the floor, screaming, had to be slow if meat was going to be really tender and red, he started on supper, slicing off a little luncheon slab from the stomach. He took down the sharp steak knife for it and cut slow so there would be lots of oozing. The grinder was clamped to the cabinet in the pantry and he put the meat in the top and tickled to see it come out the bottom in long, pink worms. It looked a bit fatty but that would make it that much tastier. She was just lying twitching there on the floor and he took out the heavy pan and threw it in. The gas flame licked up under the cast-iron bottom and he leaned back in his chair by the stove, tears in his eyes, as he peeled an onion, looking down, humming, "Ma, she's makin' eyes at me."

And then, knowing she was still alive, could hear, he knelt down where the blood was trickling from her stomach, seeping on the floor, and began to lick it up, watching her eyes, licking, smacking his lips, the smell of human flesh in the room too sweet, sickly, and he put his mouth in her stomach and began to tear at it, howling, howling.

Ma leaned forward in the seat opposite. Her breasts half-filled sacks, sagging in the cheap cotton of her dress. Prematurely gray. Worn down to the cheekbone. Dogs barked outside the bus. Something whined by the window.

A pucker recreased her wrinkled cheek. Creamy mashed potatoes whipped in with milk, butter and DDT. The kids, Mary Ellen, who was tall for thirteen; and John Jackson, just twelve; Joe Junior, the redhead, eleven; Jean Louise, ten; Josephine, nine; and the baby, Freckles, three. She dished out the lamb chops she had baked in insecticide. Pa ate so fast, trying to get finished and out the door, he didn't know what he was eating. And she just scolded the kids when they got fresh and complained. Eat it up and rejoice, that was her motto. You're lucky to get it. And they were so dopey by the time she put out the cake with bug powder and strong black coffee dosed with arsenic that it was too late to notice the taste.

She sat back and clapped her hands. It was so thrilling to see them all turning gray at the table. Freckles tried to get up from his chair and go to the kitchen, whispering, "Water, water," but she just pushed him right back in his seat. And Pa, like a fool, had gulped down three cups of coffee and was already stiff and kind of green in his chair. Mary Ellen bumped back against the wall, but it was easy to prop her up again at the table. And all the other kids fell forward, right in place.

She got up then and walked around the table, slapping their faces, good and hard. They couldn't run, or scream, or make any fuss now. When she got to Pa, she took him by the hair and started banging his head on the table, screaming at him, banged and banged, harder and harder, till she saw the blood go running out of one ear, then she started on Mary Ellen, who was right beside him, whipping her thin head down by the long braid, screaming, and she would go round and round the table, cracking them, good and hard, harder, harder, screaming.

All the night, the dark, went up in noise, lights flashing around the bus, sirens going on and off, horns, shouts, bells. With the rest of the passengers, Dora stared out the window. Beside her reared a black disk, a shining silver hub.

A boot smashed through the glass. Dora backed away just in time. A pockmarked boy with streaming hair appeared at the hole. He spit through it. The phlegm flew over Dora's shoulder and caught the dignified farmer opposite her in the eye. He sat rigid in his chair, did not move to wipe it away.

A sharp series of explosions bulleted the air. A moment later the pockmarked face whirled upside down. The motorcyclists were somersaulting, flipping their mounts right and left. Hooting, they stood up and zipped down their flies. Urine splashed against the window. A long arc came through the hole. Bucking and galloping beside the bus, one boy rose in the saddle, turned around, pulling down his Levis and showed his backside. Waving his buttocks in the air, he jumped the machine closer and closer, the white halves shimmied to the broken glass. She smelt it, what he was going to do, ramming—bull's-eye.

"Bent Fork!"

It stuck in the window, half-exploded.

Wheeling around, catcalling, the riders scattered over the fields as town roofs appeared in the headlights.

"Bent Fork!" shouted the driver.

The deputy stood in the doorway, his face narrow, handsome, moustachioed cowboy. A tall, slender man whose nose was too big.

She stumbled down the aisle with her valises.

"I'll help you, ma'am." The voice soft, reassuring. He reached out, not waiting for a reply, and took her luggage.

"Where yew goin'?" He was walking ahead of her down the main street from what she could make

"Well . . ."

"Who yew lookin' for?"

"You."

The deputy turned around, opening his mouth so she saw the long horse teeth as he burst into laughter, "Right! Right!"

She walked faster, catching up with him. "What yew want to know?"

"A boy that came from this town. I'm a reporter." She opened her purse and took out a dog-eared card.

TRUE TALES OF TERROR
accredits
Mary Ann Pure
STAFF WRITER

"Boy, yew came to the right place." His bony cheeks worked up and down. "This burg is loaded. More boobies to the square inch than anywhere in the state of Iowa. Yew use any cow-buggerin' or sheep-tiddlin' tales? Any farmer round kin pull out one of those."

He clapped her on the back, a heavy, familiar hand, and began to tell about a father and mother who pickled their kids.

"Do you remember a Star boy?"

He looked down at her, grinning. "What yew want?"

"Fingerprints, a copy . . ."

"C'mon," he said. "We'll go git it for yew."

They left the courthouse. He had opened up the doors and drawers with his keys, making copies for her and stamping them.

"Yew gonna put me in that mag?"

"Right!"

"Right! Right!" he bent over laughing, his long frame grotesque as it bent down to his knees. His comic nose rose from the road; straightening up, passing her ear, he whispered, "Where yew going to stay?"

"I'll get the bus."

"Ain't no bus."

She breathed heavily.

"Not till tomorrow morning."

"Is there somewhere to sit up?"

"C'mon, I'll fix yew up."

"Is there a hotel?"

"A roomin' house."

"It's too late."

"I got a key."

She tried to turn away, but he put his arm around her. She felt the muscles, tight as steel springs, under the blue jacket. "Yew can't stay on the street."

Her stomach began to turn, her will going soft. It was a dilapidated Victorian mansion. One window, in the highest gable, was lit, snow white. They went up the back stairs. The hinges creaked behind them as he pushed her up the rickety flight of broken steps. Dora heard raucous laughter from one of the dark rooms. It was four in the morning.

He put the valise down and opened the door, holding her with one arm. She was dragged over the threshold. The lights were on, the naked bulb in the ceiling so bright she was almost blinded. There was nothing in the room, no bed, chairs. Behind her, the door shut. She heard the key. His arm let go. She ran, to the bare wall, to the corner.

"What's the matter . . ." Her face turned away from the low drawl and she felt his strong fingers go up under her blouse, tearing the bra straps, tearing her skirt and panties down in one fistful. She put her hand down to stop him, to pull them up, and she grasped the long, hard

A white mule reared above the bathtub.

In the water Madalyn Mammothlary wallowed on her backside waiting for his plunge.

The phone rang, furious, insistent.

"Daddy!" she screamed, rising in the tub, "Daddy . . . Daddy . . ."

two

Arisen and gone forth.

I can fold the telescope, give up my window at the bank. Employed in one of our luxurious penthouse suites, you too might have caught sight of O'Dougherty, late one afternoon, the Stock Exchange gone home, a lone dot, drifting along the sidewalk currents.

> It is terrible to see how a single unclear idea, a single formula without meaning, lurking in a young man's head, will sometimes act like an obstruction of the brain. . . . Many a man has cherished for years as his hobby some vague shadow of an idea, too meaningless to be positively false: he has, nevertheless, passionately loved it, has made it his companion by day and by night, and has given to it his strength and his life, leaving all other occupations for its sake, and in short has lived with it and for it, until it has become, as it were, flesh of his flesh and bone of his bone: and then he has waked up some bright morning to find it gone, clean vanished away like the beautiful Melusina of the fable, and the essence of his life gone with it. I have myself known such a man, and who can tell how many histories of circle squarers, metaphysicians, astrologers and what not, may not be told in the old German story?
>
> —*How to Make Your Ideas Clear* by Charles Pierce

Yet here at the bank we have feeling for that fellow. Investments go beyond coin in the vaults, figures juggled in the ledger. If trade, policy abroad, war, lie in our domain, why not domestic horror? We finance the movies of Hollywood, Presidential campaigns. Our fees buy the best consultants in the land. Shall we then be ignorant of drama, catharsis? We have need of magic, of the art of the soothsayer, of what not. Is it still unthinkable—out of evil might come good?

And we have our own sanity to think of. How dull to scrape and smooth the endless blocks of this gray edifice, mounting higher and higher, so that, growing weary of the skill of my accountants, lawyers, politicians, the incisive truths of my analyst, I find myself here on the window ledge, scraping my knees, leaning out farther and farther, oh, if man could. . . .

Ah, I see him stepping out. O'Dougherty throws his tweed coat open, the sharp nose turns up, breathing, he flies dizzily into the New York air.

"Tonight! Tonight!" he cried to the empty street. He sprang into the air, elated and jerking with nervous excitement, the telegram shook in his hand.

The word. The sense of power made him giddy. The air was alive, electric. Across the street, a cowpath of New Amsterdam, in a canyon between towering banks, the tiny graveyard of an eighteenth century church survived, bloomed with time-worn markers. He could smell the nails rusting in its melting earth. Ancient country churchyard arose in the moist air, surged into the street.

O'Dougherty spun around on the sidewalk, years whirled away. He circled across the street, bolted up on the iron spears of the cemetery fence.

Muskets, pistols, harquebus, blunderbuss, waving—fired. Drums beating, a crowd pours down the narrow avenue, dirt underfoot. Smell of powder, sweat, hysteria swelling from every side lane. Dispossessed, disgruntled colony, small merchants, hungry farmers, idle artisans, half-breed Indians, Negro servants, dammed to the second story, Leisler's door. Lead us! Lead us! Fists on the oak door, arms, angry, knotting; ropes fastened, civic edifice. Pull! Pull!

O'Dougherty leaped off the fence, sprang to the sidewalk and resumed his walk. The paper crumpled in his hand.

"Jesus," he exclaimed. "Jesus."

A seed had taken root within him. A grain. A mustard. He laughed. Yet felt it put out root, spread and gather strength, promise in the warmth of that mild March evening. Eighteen, he felt eighteen. On a scrap, a single, small secret; in his palm he felt the bulk, the weight of America. It swayed in his hand.

O'Dougherty, at the limits of the continent, stared into the blue. Ringed with missiles, rockets, nuclear bolts, O'Dougherty. The United States. O'Dougherty. The Western world, O'Dougherty. "No!" he cried. Dreams kept whispering in his ears. "No!"

D. O'Dougherty, free-lance writer, uncovered, *story of the century,* yesterday. Startled America awoke, *glaring six-inch headlines.* A special session of Congress called, deal with events revealed under O'Dougherty byline. Expected to testify, a joint session, House and Senate, before nightfall. The President with Mr. O'Dougherty, in earnest conversation, could not be reached for comment, press secretary promised fresh copy in the morning. Hinted, O'Dougherty at work, several other national scandals, public, breathless, waiting, news to break. Special assignment Mr. O'Dougherty, from White House, unconfirmed.

Relatively unknown (to the general public), D. O'Dougherty has enjoyed a distinguished reputation for almost a decade among a small but important group of New York editors. Not only have his articles appeared from time to time in the *avant-garde* periodicals downtown, but a number of important trade magazines have enjoyed his services. He has published in *Refrigerator Services, Woolen Knits, Civil Service News, Retired People's Daily, Rent a Car Travel Guide,* and *The Sales Bulletin.* His byline was featured in *American Museums, Insurance Times, Business Executives Annual, Furniture Monthly,* and *Jobber Topics.* He worked for a number of years as a contributor to *Collier's Encyclopedia,* the *Encyclopedia Americana, World Book, Current Biography, Funk and Wagnall's Dictionary,* etc., etc.

Year in and year out his copy has excited, charmed, interested, filled up column after column, grim, gray type, copy, factual copy, reams and reams of copy, dead, dead prose. Paper, paper, his rooms were cluttered with piles. *Refrigerator Services, Retired People's Daily, Funk and Wagnall's Dictionary,* his biography. Reams and reams, *O'Dougherty, His Life.* Forty, paper, paper. He was now forty. Still on the treadmill rolling him forward through those jobs. Nothing, he had brought forth nothing, wind, conceived wind, wind.

O'Dougherty stared into the grim vacancy of Foley Square.

Nothing, not a building. Bare space where city blocks had stood. Silence where the crowds had hustled.

He stood in the midst of deserted cobbles.

A gap, savage, scooped out in the center of the city.

Nothing.

He crossed the cobbles to a cracked sidewalk skirting the wasteland, walked with care. Sections had buckled, crumbled away, trembling in the upheavals of the hole which was now invisible, circumscribed by a wooden fence just above eye level. A few hundred feet down, for no apparent purpose, was a gate, a frame of two-by-fours covered with chicken wire. The opening for the grade down was farther along.

O'Dougherty, his black pumps flexing and snapping on the uneven sidewalk, picked his way toward the barrier. He squeezed in front of a large Mack diesel. The gate was locked.

He pushed. The beams creaked but it would not give. Inserting the toe of his pump in the chicken wire, he climbed. Swinging himself over, he slid down inside the fence. He turned, faced across the three-acre abyss.

A few feet away the ground fell. Without slope it dropped hundreds of feet, bottomless. Down, down, O'Dougherty took a step forward, another, another. The earth crumbled away as he inched his toe over the edge. He was queasy between the legs. It was a terrible drop; the hole awesome in the shadow of dusk, the bottom deeper.

To go down, into the tomb, dark, grave.

He swayed, his head giddy, clutched at the chicken wire, looked up.

A shadow glided against darkening silver, drifted on a downward current of air in wide arcs, floated around and around hardly seeming to drop in its circle. A dot, blurring, darker and darker, until a barely discernible shape hung on the edge of the arc, slipping along.

O'Dougherty began to turn, his fingers tearing loose of the wire. Up, up, the enlarging dot above him, soared down around him, pulling him up into flight; hung for a moment, motionless in focus, a great bird. O'Dougherty's fingers free of the wire, he stepped forward, forward, into the wings of the bird he stepped.

Exploding in feathers, reeking from the sky, the hot smell of the bird's filth in his nose, he reeled, trying to hold his balance, buffeted, the powerful wings knocking him. The rim crumbled. He fell to his knees, blind, one hand on his eyes, trying to shield them from the talons, his other clutching dirt, pebbles, snatching at broken roots to pull himself up to the gate, sliding. The bird above him grunting, deep, malicious clucks. He tangled his fingers in the wire, dragged himself through the foul air.

Sharp, stinging, the beak razored his fingers.

He lunged, one-handed, trying to batter the thing off.

It clucked softly, a sigh in its throat. He saw its talons white with its own excrement, the raw red neck, a mucous flesh, and the eye, gleaming, hideous. It lifted itself into the sky, a throb of the wingspread, only the smell of his own terror behind, his fingers smarting, bleeding on the chicken wire.

He clung to the fence. There was nothing. He looked up. Nothing. Sky, a pit below.

Slowly he lifted the scuffed toe of his pump, inserted it in a loop, began to pull himself, furtive, starting at every move up the wire.

Outstretched on a bull's-eye, he spun.

His hand lashed against the chicken wire. He pushed his back against it, pinned the gate to the ground, looked up. A clear, chalk sky.

Twisting around, O'Dougherty swung free for a second, caught the wire with his hand and foot. He hoisted himself up, felt the beam bite into his stomach and clambered over the top. His fingers were raw, crusted with blood. He fell to the ground, looked up again and, reassured, slipped out behind the Mack truck.

He began to run along the broken sidewalk, into shadows, his father, apoplectic, tumbling purple-faced in the parlor chair, pronouncing judgment. A load of shit. Playing with himself. Cut the goddamn thing off. Fuckin' idiot.

Forty years, no, no! He ran faster. His mother, shrunken, rose a skeleton, eaten up in the hospital bed, before it fell apart, shaking the bone finger, "Don't, don't."

In a torn trench coat, unshaven, socks around his ankles, he ran toward him out of a subway hole, howling, shouting in Latin. A bum, a wasted life, napping on the steps of the public library, talking about Nietzsche, Schopenhauer, Saint Thomas Aquinas. A Boston common intellectual cadging drinks, coffee, doughnuts. Digging graves for a living. Hoping to talk some girl out of high school into seconds of respect. A broken pencil in his pocket. He ran toward him, out of the subway hole, howling.

O'Dougherty collided. The force of the blow staggered him, he clutched his forehead—a telephone booth.

Wincing, he remembered. The call, he had promised as soon as it came. He pushed through the half-open accordion door and tore the receiver off its hook.

A dime rang in the box. He dialed, heard it ring, hung up.

O'Dougherty stepped slowly out of the booth. The air, sweet, flushed his cheeks as he walked.

There was no traffic. An accident on the East River Drive or the strange hour of dusk at the tip of the island between office closing and evening entertainment had emptied the streets. The square he walked into was deserted and an unexpected flow of spring intoxicated him.

He was at the foot of two temples of stone, the squat form of the state supreme court and the dull, rising square of the federal court. He had overshot the subway. It was behind him on a little concrete island planted with shrubs.

He looked up. Both buildings were stained by years of city air. Their pillared facades were mottled brown, as if generations had spit on them. In a corner of the federal building where they had begun to sandblast the grit, a white granite shone.

The yellowed stone of the state court was untouched. It sat on the square, an old derbied politician, a face of tobacco.

"Argue!" O'Dougherty shouted. "Argue!"

His voice echoed back from the arch of the roofs. The last syllable rose instead of dying away, rebounded, swept up again to the portico, ascended from the wide, sweeping steps. "Aaaa-aahhhhh . . . uuuuuuuuuuuuu . . . aaaaaaahhhh . . . uuuuuuuuu. . . ."

The bodies of men in rags rose on the stone rungs of the court. The sweepings of the Bowery, they had drifted down in the dusk and crept onto the staircase to nestle in the hard granite cots formed of the steps. Bundled in old overcoats, blanketed in dirty underwear, they crouched in open coverts on the Hall of Justice, sleeping, half-awake, muttering. It was they who had echoed his drunken cry, rising, nodding in rags, to his shout.

Unshaven, red-eyed, a few staggered a step or two downward, came to a stop, their momentum stumbling in apathy. O'Dougherty turned away.

"Uuuuuuuu . . ." he heard behind him a single voice, strained, hoarse.

A bandaged cavity of flesh thrust into O'Dougherty's face. The man's features eaten out of recognition, scar over uneven bone contracted, knotting into a hole. "Uuuuuu . . . uuuuu. . . ." O'Dougherty stepped backward in the smell of whiskey, urine, tripped, fell

A hand touched his leg. It slipped into O'Dougherty's trouser, reaching up. He jumped, jamming his legs together. Jesus! Clothes swarming cockroaches, the webbed hole dripped saliva, opening wider, wider, wet, pink flesh. It touched his face, opening. The bone pushed up. Nauseous, twisting, he threw off the creature. Free, he ran toward the subway, hands beating his pockets, frenzied, for a token. The vagrant followed, limping behind, moaning.

O'Dougherty clattered down the stairs, reaching the teller's booth, made change and hurried through the iron turnstile. The train roared into the station.

He threw himself on the moving cars, running alongside them, calling to be let in. Only as the squeal of brakes died away he heard behind him in the hush, uuuuuuu, uuuuuuuu, and swinging around, backed into the opening doors, seeing, himself screaming at the turnstile.

The train left an empty trench coat swarming with rats.

Plump, white globes. Nervous, upset, excited, Dora seized them, tugging at their long rose tips, weighing them back and forth in her palms, feeling their bulk grow agitated, erect, tense, expectant, almost jumping in the fresh March air pouring through the open windows of her apartment.

She shook the bath water from her hair. Her tits were getting bigger. Every year they weighed more, stretching her bras, straining the halter straps, rising up and pushing out of her sweater whenever she got that crazy rush of hunger that was pulling, tugging at her now. She twisted, twisted the limp flesh of the nipples until they hardened into iron. She squeezed them so that she almost screamed.

"Oh shit, shit." She slapped them and began to cry. They were coming. She knew it. Again and again and again, she dug her fingernails into the soft flesh, raking it until blood flowed in the scratches.

She shook her head to drive them off, wet snakes whipped about her shoulders, damp black strands of hair. O'Dougherty would be here soon. Daniel. Daniel. I'm a good girl, look.

She went down on her knees, mumbling Hebrew, repeating the same prayer over and over under her breath, a charm, a spell, white magic.

Get dressed, she told herself. Go ahead. Get something on. Bra, slip, panties, dress, hurry up.

Turning, she crawled a step toward the bedroom, and the cold spring air swept in, over her, under her, around, spinning, tumbling, O God, God, I can't help it. She reared up and rolled backward, slumping down to the linoleum.

O, O.

The floor was rubbery under her buttocks, damp, spots of bath water. Down her legs spread goose pimples apart, slowly to receive the breeze, a tongue of ice, half-thawing in it, tickled, pricked her.

A hoof, black, gelatinous, rested on the windowsill.

A second.

A fleshy pink chin, wiry with bristles, edged over.

Two long ears upthrust, then the enormous snout, chopped off, blunt, obscene shovel.

It stared, savage, stupid, an elongated, chinless face, nostrils stuffed with hair, cheeks smooth as a female's.

Her knees trembled in the air.

The porker's jaw dropped open.

Uneven rows of curling, misshaped teeth showed. She could smell the rotten stuff of the alley below in that lewd, amazed breath. It had been rooting in the bags of week-old orange peels, coffee grinds, egg shells, the dirt at the bottom of the air shaft, years of mop water, slop buckets, urine, damp rubbers, the membrane of unborn babies, fetus, the gaping mouth dripped.

Slime spattered the linoleum. Dora's thighs were sliding.

The pig began to push itself up through the window frame. Grunting, squealing, it tried to squeeze between the sill and the edge of the open window. Waving the massive head back and forth inside the room, it wedged first one forefoot, then the other in. Gasping, flushing, a red to apoplexy in its face, it elbowed, strained, scraped through the stiff frame, the great blossom of the picnics, bruised, splotched, inching.

O God, God.

The pig slid forward, fiery, awful, enormous.

Stuck. Halfway in.

Dora stretched her thighs back. She dug her heels into the floor, pushing herself apart until the leg muscles taut, knotted, a dancer's split.

The pig's face was venous, broken out in spots of purple. It did not grunt or squeal, but grinding its teeth, shook the window frame, trying to force its spine down into its belly.

The bone would not bulge. Its back bit into the splintering lintel.

Caught, stopped by the beam, the pig turned, twisted between the rigid struts, trying to roll upon its side, rasping its flesh. It leaned halfway, neither up nor down, screwed at an angle, pushing.

A trembling mass of pork butted in the frame, thrusting, thrusting, forcing itself into the room.

Dora was bolted to the floor.

A bolt's head, a rod, the body trembled, palpitating.

All of it. The length of it. The unclean body, bloodshot eyes, sharp whiskers, teeth, tusks, hooves, tail. The thing come into her. Her flesh, her guilt dissolved in streams of sickening, sweet terror.

O, O, slowly the pig began to slip back through the window as she drew her thighs together, its bulk tumbled from the wooden lip, soft, soundless, it crashed below.

The floor was sticky under her. She lifted her body off the linoleum, buttocks smacking, first one, then the other. Lady found in East Side dive devoured by porker. Pieces all over the place. Half asleep, Dora took a step toward the bathtub. What was it doing there? Police piece together pieces. She turned the faucets on. Water. Water. Puddle on the floor. To the lab. Analysis finds! She watched the bath tumble into the porcelain tub.

Impotent. Drained. Still waters. Temptation. Cut.

Dora bent down and jerked the faucets shut. Cut! Would he do it? She had tried. She had, once. All by herself, after the flight from California. Scared shitless, she called. Called! Machine guns fired from the windows of passing black sedans. Each night, razors in hand, rapists, murderers, crawled through her window. They waited in the cellar beneath, a tub of wet cement. On the river a ferry wailed the hour of appointment. Strangers winked, giving the password.

She changed names, apartments, jobs. She sank into the New York slums, hid for months in the three tiny rooms, peeling plaster, no stove, refrigerator, slinking out at night for groceries. Only they knew. She saw it, felt it everywhere. Desperate, she surfaced. Come and get me! she screamed into the airshaft, Come and get me!

Come and get me, in the grocery store, on the street, into traffic. She was going crazy, she knew. Ready to commit herself. Cut!

Oh, no! Not that way. Too easy. Come and get me. She calmed down. Got a job again. Started going out. She would get them. Only she couldn't do it by herself. O'Dougherty!

She pulled him down off the railing. Forty-year-old virgin. He walked her home, a long bump straining the fabric of his pants. She said goodbye, her hand, accidentally, brushing.

He called, excited. Let's go out, anywhere, wild, extravagant. The first date she let him put his hand up her dress. Then, for two weeks she wouldn't speak to him on the phone. Again she went out with him. Invited him in to her place, took off her sweater, complaining it was hot. She sat in her bra, talking to him, slapping his hands away as he reached across the table, time after time.

A gentleman, he rose with offended dignity after half an hour and walked toward the door. Dora got up, too. She followed him. "Goodnight," she said.

O'Dougherty, standing in the doorway, one eye on her breasts, the muscles in his cheeks twitching, managed a smile. "It's been nice."

A long silence. She felt his hands trembling toward her tits. "Young lady," he said, clearing his throat. "I can play games, too."

He wheeled, stiff-backed, and started for the stairs.

"Daniel," she called. "Would you . . ."

He stopped.

In the open door of her apartment, Dora turned her back on him. She hiked up her skirt and white slip. Her hand, coy, touched her ass, pulled the black panties off, tugged them down. She heard his footsteps, felt his lips.

Spinning, "Enough!" she slammed the door in his face. He banged on it for minutes.

"Stick it through the keyhole."

Mr. O'Dougherty retired.

A three-day silence. He called at midnight. Assured her he could take a joke. Laughing, asked if they could meet again.

She agreed to visit him. On top of an old gingerbread commercial building in an abandoned suite of offices at the tip of Manhattan overlooking the Hudson and East Rivers. Elegant scrolls in the facade. No elevators. Half the floors empty. His rooms were dusty. Stained prints of old steamships, cracked glass in gilt frames, hung on the walls. No furniture. His cot was in the corner of one of the offices. And on an overturned wooden crate, a silver-plate tea service shone with delicate white china cups. A bottle of Irish whiskey also sat on the crate.

Dora smiled sadly. Her naked body shivered in the chill of a sudden draft. Pinpoints prickled over her. She put a hand on her thigh. It glowed.

O'Dougherty grinned. "I was afraid you wouldn't come." Dressed in an old double-breasted tuxedo, black tie, he motioned her to a cracking leather chair. They had their tea with a slice of strawberry shortcake he produced from a paper bag. One of his socks was curling around an ankle. His neck was thick. She saw the middle-age paunch as he leaned forward.

"Dignity," he whispered. "I preserve it."

She hid her grimace.

"A gentleman, the press," he chuckled, stirring the thick lump of comb honey in his tea. It was a smoky Tartar leaf. On an abandoned desk which served as his kitchen cabinet there were a dozen boxes, jasmine, mint, Darjeeling. The smoke from the tea cup rose in her nostrils.

"You think I'm a bum?"

"No," she whispered. Not again. Her hand wandered finger by finger to the first strands of hair, touched them, entangled, twisting in the bush between her legs, rank, acrid.

"No?" staring past her. "Look at my generation. Corrupted in their jobs, their security, their families. Corrupted by helplessness, between one war they remember, one they slogged through or evaded, one more, terrible, too terrible to think about, that always threatens. Not their corporate charade. Not their dignity."

"What?"

O'Dougherty rose in his seat. "Listen . . . I've eaten with old classmates, Rockefellers, Cabots, Morgans, they don't have it. That money is tied up, locked into the charade. They're more timid, uneasy than anyone. Their dignity is stuffed, mummified. Energy, Blake said that's what it's about, life. Power!"

"For what?"

"Evil!"

O'Dougherty laughed. He looked into her eyes. "To destroy oneself."

"Why?" Her finger slid along the crack.

"The flame upon the night." O'Dougherty doubled his fists and knocked on his breast. "My own resinous heart." He took a step toward her. "To wake up, to live, to pass with dignity. 'Reason not the need, our basest beggars, in the poorest things, superfluous, but for true *need.*' "

The color started in his pale face. "I'm the son of a politician, it's my heartbeat, need, the public pulse is on my fingertips. Not what you say when some stranger knocks on the door, takes the neighborhood poll. What you dream as your wife rolls, the other side of the bed. What makes you flame, forbidden, unclean, upon the night."

She felt the heat bubble.

"I know what they need. Not just the corporation men, but in diners, garages, behind the counters of small stores, going bankrupt, trapped, sleepwalking, leading two, three, four, infinite lives, under the surface, after the lights are out, the charade over. Praying for their nightmares to come to life. Praying for something to come along and smash all the sanities. Praying for breakdown, madness, horror, catastrophe."

The hole sucked at the tip of her hand, sinking.

He lurched forward. "I, among them, O'Dougherty, son of chieftains, destroyers, obstructors, cattle robbers, barn burners, a king, a ravisher, rapist." He bent down, his lips flushed, ears flaming.

"Stop!" she screamed. "Don't touch me!" Hysterical, kicking, scratching in his embrace. As he drew back, frightened, the tears streamed down her face. She sobbed into the folds of cracked leather.

"Look," he said. "I'm sorry.

"All right, I'm a bum.

"Dora. I'm nothing. Forget it. Don't see me again. Please. Don't cry. I was just going crazy. I've got nothing. No prospects, accomplishments, nothing, dreams. I'm bitter, stupid."

Her face was deep in the chair. Her shoulders heaved.

"Jesus, please don't." He began to cry. "I'm desperate. I've got to get something to hold on to. A bottle, drugs. I'm going to sink into the gutter. You're just a girl, a baby. You don't know how it is.

"All right, you guessed it, I'm a pervert." He sank to his knees, his hands in his face, "Mary, Mother of God, help me. Help me."

Dora looked at him.

She got up and walked over. "It's not you," she whispered, her voice shaking.

She began to tell.

O'Dougherty was staggered. He listened in shock.

". . . police sergeant . . . hospital . . . Los Angeles. . . ." Only bits of the story. He was squeezing his fists tight, unable to stand still now, jerking.

"Where?" he thrashed out as she stopped talking. The tears were dry on her face. "How?" She was afraid again.

"I'll help! I'll help!" he cried. "Tell me more!" He was telling himself.

She dropped a crumb or two more. He bobbed down and bussed her. "It's my story, ours." He hugged her.

"Dora! It's incredible. Please!"

No, the rest when they were ready to move.

He paced the floor, making sense of what he knew.

They had to have fingerprints. He walked up and down. They had to prove it. A buyer, they had to find the right one. A liberal newspaper that would pay and give the story national coverage. "Incredible," he muttered, trying to smile.

Fingerprints. Two sets. She went for one. "No, no!" She went. The paper, the buyer, he promised, would get the other. She came back. Not yet. They were having trouble. The regular channels were blocked. Private detectives couldn't get near him.

"Why not just the story?"

No, he wanted it to be more than that, a statement, a case, some final definition, an airtight trap.

Proof! Proof!

"Let him prove it!"

"What if it isn't . . . ?"

Dora turned to the window. It faced a blank wall, yet beyond it you could see the city.

A year now they had been waiting, hanging, watching Star, watching the stake going higher and higher. The story was worth a fortune.

Would he do it? Would he?

He couldn't write. He couldn't act. He was one of them. Insidious, they had tied her to an impotent, a eunuch.

"You bastard!" she shouted. He had promised today, a telegram. A call. It was too late, you bastard. I'm going crazy. I'm snapping. It was coming up in her again, jerking, tingling, twisting.

She was standing in front of the open window. Look at me,

you Peeping Toms! There was the metropolis, spires of steel, stone, sharp peak after peak. Wet between the legs, she wanted to climb on them, jump on them, bury them in her, the whole thrust of the city, overwhelm it in soft flesh.

She screamed.

Outside, in the gray industrial sky, a faint glimmer struck a spark in the darkening dullness. Night descended on the city.

Twinkle. Twinkle.

"Aaaaaaaaaaaaah!" O'Dougherty ground his teeth into the cry, stifling it, as he rocketed through the darkness. Inside, the glare of bulbs lighted the passengers into anonymity.

His behind trembled on plastic. The bum—his thoughts recoiled. Whiskey, beer, tobacco, odor in the car of Lower Manhattan bars, faces of his father's followers, on the steps of the State House a governor took the oath of office, stamping in the January cold; old men pulling at his father's coat, whispering it would be him in that place soon. A bitter St. Patrick's Day blew through the open windows in a long, black limousine, his father leaning out to wave at ladies, kids, white-haired gentlemen, bowler all decked in green; ribbons, shirts, ties, streamers. Emerald cloth streamed, the coming of spring in the chill March air. And from the car Daniel saw in the midst of the happy faces pushing forward to get a look, a man thrusting himself out of the bundle on the sidewalk, all gums.

O'Dougherty brought his hands to his face. Think of Dora's place, objects, solid ones, chairs rescued from the street. One, two, three, four; broken springs, rotted stuffing, smell of insecticide, dead roaches. Dora insisted they were antiques. He fixed them and the table snatched from the garbage. Chipped plastic top, peeling paint; scrubbing the tar off, he screwed the wobbly legs tight. Took his reward in the tiny tub by the kitchen sink.

In the other room she lay on the bed. Hot, soapy, lying back, trying to relax, he soaked in the parody, man of the house. Teasing silently, she moved, her swollen breasts made the bed creak. Looking down at his flesh, half-erect, the white belly bubbling sadly in the eddying waters, stared up at him, a blank, opening.

"All right!" shouted O'Dougherty, getting to his feet. The passengers looked up, startled, the agreement of silence shattered.

Embarrassed, O'Dougherty tried to ignore the stares. He squinted at a map of the subway system. The car rattling, his finger jerked tracing the night's route to the stadium. The Continentals would be heading out there soon. Black caps dotting the crowds of New York, their conversation hummed in the back of bars, restaurants, building lobbies, buzzing of flies.

Zzzzzzzzzzum!

The car jolted to the side. It threw O'Dougherty off balance and the slam of the brakes staggered him. He almost fell as the subway doors opened and he stumbled onto the platform.

It was deserted. The train began to leave the station. O'Dougherty steadied himself, looked around. Alone, except for a black back at the other end. He recognized the uniform. They hardly ever traveled out of company, two or three. Like nuns, so it was strange to see the lone uniform under the high, bleak ceiling.

O'Dougherty whistled a few bars to cheer himself up. "It's a long way to Tipperary . . ." morbid echo down the long platform. The figure in black turned around and began to walk toward him.

Flies, locusts, O'Dougherty felt the telegram pressed into his palm, a wad. If the figure moving toward him knew, the empty station, the silent electric rail, below, a million volts, aaaaaaaaaaaaah!

He danced on his toes. Looked up, started.

It was a woman. Close-cropped hair, butch cut, the masculine uniform, pants and jacket, about his height.

O'Dougherty could tell by the rouge, lipstick, long eyelashes, a member of the Ladies' Auxiliary. She walked with an inviting wobble. Stopped a few feet away from him, turned the other way.

Obviously waiting. O'Dougherty smelled liquor. Pretty, despite the outfit. Out with the boys for a bang. What would it be like to slip the black pants off? Push in the black forest of bitchiness, clamped. Down in the basement bar behind the swinging doors, ladies' room, showing her muff.

Why abandon her here in the city? Novelty worn off, searching for new game. A bit flat-chested. Still, nice to chew, pouting little breasts. Have her on his cot by the bookcase, under Plato, Milton.

Her brassiere lost under the bed, slender legs, O'Dougherty rocked them slowly apart, buried himself stiff in a soft heart.

A flush of pleasure, a sidelong glance for detail, O'Dougherty seduced, triumphed. His imagination was spinning to the aftermath. Both of them, her tall, nude body perched on the cot edge, poring over Milton. He, discovering in this discarded village trash an excitable, inquiring mind. Her reformation, gradual entrance into the ranks of culture, education. Long, happy marriage. . . . O'Dougherty had to pause, accuse himself of drunkenness. Must be inhaling her fumes.

His lust ebbed. Emboldened by exhaustion, self-contained, above temptation, he

She was staring.

The lipstick laid on too heavily, the rouge caked, false eyelashes. A streak of ill temper ran through her features, twisting the smile. Something familiar about her, cunning mouth. Unused to the city, doesn't want to make herself a fool.

A smile crept onto O'Dougherty's face. The lady grinned back boldly. O'Dougherty's masculine cockiness challenged:

"Hello?"

"Hi!" Her voice was high, falsetto.

"You going to the convention?"

"Yew from New York?" the twang Midwestern. "This shur is a dir-ty city."

"Lot of people live in it."

"Full of dir-ty people, too." She took a step toward him. "Hangin' round this kinda place, yew never know who yew gonna meet."

"What do you mean?"

"Yew know what I'm talkin' 'bout." Her face distorted by a knowing look. "Yew know what kind."

O'Dougherty flushed. Tight-lipped, he asked, "Where are your friends?"

The lady took a step back, answered gruffly, "They ain't here."

"They get lost?" solicitous, feeling stupid.

"Oh, yeeeaaah."

"That's too bad. You know where you are?"

"The subway?" she asked, mockingly.

"I thought you might be lost."

"Yew the one sounds lost."

O'Dougherty shivered. Some other people had wandered down the stairs at the other end of the station. In the distance, the steady clanking of a train grew louder. The female Continental had not turned her eyes from him. She stared greedily. "Yew from New York?"

What the hell, O'Dougherty laughed. "Where are you from?"

Her green eyes glittered, the high voice cracking, "What d'yew care?"

The train was beating its way along the track into the station. "You have an interesting face. I'm always curious."

"Yeeeeaaah. I like yew, too." There was a pause. "Yew gonna get this train?"

Her tongue flicked out, coy, pink. O'Dougherty felt the train brake on its steel slides to a standstill.

"No," he answered, shaken. It was his connection.

The doors of the subway opened. A handful of passengers walked out, the car receiving a smaller one in return. He stood motionless, opposite the young lady on the slender concrete island, listening as the car left the dock, gliding away into the silent passageways, hearing his heartbeat. She waited until the last whisper of train and footsteps had echoed into a tense hush. Then leaning forward, asked, "Where?"

O'Dougherty's heart jumped. It leaped again and his eyes glazed, a veil of tears, his head steaming. His stomach turned. Jesus. He was moving closer to her, a few inches away, the muscles tight in her face, her knee crooked suggestively touching his own. Her hands, red fingernails, reached for . . . The ball of paper tightened in his hand. The dark red rose, the opening flesh, her mouth toward his. A moment in which he had played with a younger sister, flesh between her legs, musky, slippery. O'Dougherty's face streaked with white beads, stinging, the woman's mouth gaudy. His legs were giving way, her knee, hands digging into his arm, holding him close, feeling her moist lips brush his cheek, wet upon his mouth. A train was coming in again along the track. Her leg between his, one hand across his rear. His mouth, her tongue curling, both heard the train. A dark shape slid forward. She dropped her arms, stepped back.

Out of the top window of the car opposite, four heads.

"Hey, what's this shit?"

"You ain't bein' true!"

"Kissy wissy, kissy wissy."

O'Dougherty recognized the narrow black caps. The faces grinned. Kiss after kiss they threw from the window, smacking their lips, salacious. A four-headed monster, purring, sucking.

The first, bald, fat, dripping. "Doh-rathee!" cried the gleaming, sweaty pinkness, "Staht shakin' it."

The face beside it shook with laughter, deeply tanned, lantern-jawed, glistening, a thin coat of suntan oil spread from brow to throat. The beach scent, the hair under the cap neatly groomed, a male model, "Hey, pal, peeky booh."

"Peeky booky. . . ." Drops caught the light on the priest's lower lip. Quick, frightened eyes, yellow, malicious, darted back and forth as he oohed and aahed, glee under his tongue, caught in his teeth, drooled over his lips.

"Dooky dicky . . ." giggling, "Tricky ficky . . . licky sticky . . . stucky muck . . . lucky. . . ."

The last face, lean, cruel, made a victory sign over the father's head, two-fingered.

All four burst into hilarity, suggestive noises.

"Yew bastards," Dorothy called out.

"Sucky ducky!" the priest shouted. They roared, swelled through the narrow box of the upper window, genies, oozing up from under the city, its rusting pipes, sewers.

"Hootsie tootsie! Hotsssy tohtsssssssy."

Hissing, the mouths slipped out of the window into the thick air of the underground, a fetid breath. The train buckles, heaves. The walls of the long tunnel twist before it. The lady, her gross friends, all float around in front of O'Dougherty. Under his clothes, dissolving, turning naked in a circle. A knife pricks upward between his legs. The telegram fluttered from his hand.

O'Dougherty snatched at the yellow fragment. He felt the sweat stabbing in the corners of his eyes. The back bedroom, his older sister lifting up a silk nightgown, letting him put his finger in her crack, clammy. The children next door, twigs tight in the stink buds of each other's behinds. An abandoned caboose, the railroad yards, boys forcing him to show his thing, an excited circle.

"Ihtsy titsy!" cried the Boston voice.

Dorothy, in a charade of offense, puffed out her chest, bunching the black cloth of her jacket up to her breasts, thrust the crumpled folds forward as if to suckle her friends.

"Whoooooooooo hoooooooooh!"

"Get a load of that!"

"Ihtsy pitssy!"

She looked at him. "Yew wanna come? We're gonna have a lot of fun."

O'Dougherty stumbled, muttered, "Keeping an appointment. . . ."

Dorothy arched her heavily blacked eyebrows. O'Dougherty shrank.

"All right, honey." She swung her rear, walked toward the doors of the subway.

"Who's yah friend, Doh-rathee?"

"Bring him along."

"We got room."

The voices were submerged in the resumed purring of the engines. Dorothy, in the entrance of the train, turned around again, faced O'Dougherty. Her hand dropped to her pants fly. Zipped it down.

Something popped out.

The air swarmed with insects. It was a king-size hot dog. Waved at him before the doors rolling together closed on it.

O'Dougherty tumbled into the channel.

Aaaaaaaaaaaah, caught himself, stared.

They disappeared through a whirling hole.

A knock on the door.

"Who is it?"

A muffled but familiar sound.

"Come in."

The long face appeared in the doorway, the latch, as usual, open. Dora, combing her long black hair in the mirror, saw O'Dougherty's reflection. "It's the big day!" she shouted.

He did not reply but, walking to the tub, sat on its edge. Dora turned around, "No?"

O'Dougherty sighed and looked away.

"You got the telegram?"

"Yes," he mumbled.

"He'll buy?"

"When we drop the papers off."

"Is it open now?"

"All night, all day," said O'Dougherty, shifting his buttock. "They probably won't break it till tomorrow. They'll put it in the Sunday magazine, too."

"Money in the bank then?" she asked, dogged.

"If someone else doesn't break it." O'Dougherty showed his teeth in a ghastly smile.

"What the hell is the matter with you?" snapped Dora.

"Ah've got troubles," sang O'Dougherty. "You've got troubles. The whole world, it's got troubles."

Dora grimaced. O'Dougherty was waving his long legs in the air. "Higher, higher," she said. "Show a little toussie."

"Wheeee!" he cried on the edge of the tub, kicking into the air. Dora whistled.

There was a crash. Two legs rocked feebly, dangled, broken sticks over the porcelain edge.

She looked down. He was sitting in the middle of a puddle, biting his lip. "You have a cushion?"

"Go in the other room. Lie on the bed."

Picking himself up in the slippery tub, he slid back on his rear. "Owwwwwww!" Dora watched him put a hand under his seat, stroking the flesh. "A cup of tea?"

"Do we have time?" she asked.

"It only takes an hour to get there. Set the alarm. He won't come on until midnight."

"We could drop off the papers."

"Afterward."

"Why?"

"Behold." O'Dougherty gripped the sides of the bathtub and slowly raised himself up. Drops of water dripped from his pants seat. "The Res-ee-rection."

Dora didn't smile. He looked at her sadly. "I seem to be wet. You wouldn't have a spare pair of underwear?"

"Sure, the bottom drawer, that's where I keep my jockey shorts."

O'Dougherty grinned, stepping out of the tub, trekked toward the bedroom leaving a trail of water on the linoleum.

She heard him intone, "And tear the heart out of that side." His voice swelled, "and bear that beating heart away. And then did all the Muses sing, of Magnus Annus in the spring, as though God's death were but a . . . play."

"What's the matter?" Dora asked, stepping into the doorway of the bedroom. "Bad dreams?"

O'Dougherty looked at her.

"Hey!" shouted Dora. "You bastard, get up. You're soaking the bed."

He stood up. His pants had left a wet blotch in the middle of the blanket.

"Take 'em off."

Meekly he complied, unhitching the natty red elastic belt that held up his dignified blue pants. They slumped to his heels, revealing boxer shorts, elastic bands around his tall black socks.

He slipped off his shorts. Stood naked, gangling, his suit jacket not quite covering the private parts. Dora looked at him for a moment, then walked back into her kitchen, took the drying bath towel off the back of her toilet door and threw it into the other room.

"Call up now," she shouted back. Stalking over to the hotplate that served for her stove, Dora picked up a large aluminum kettle from the cold burner, shook it. Water sloshed. She put it down again and flicked the switch on. A red glow underspread the kettle.

"They thrice presented me with a kingly crown!" A toga of orange and blue stripes appeared in the doorway. "Which I did thrice refuse." A long arm jabbed the air. "Was this ambition?"

"Ambition should be made of sterner stuff," replied Dora.

"My friends," said O'Dougherty, appearing, leaning against the door jamb. "We are met to consider whether this nation, conceived in liberty, dedicated, shall perish from the earth. We are met on a portion of the battlefield, to dedicate, to consecrate, to hallow the blood, the crimson, steaming blood of the lamb. The curly white lamb. The innocent! I call upon you now, ye faithful, dry your tears, upraise your spears, and march. March on. *Allons, enfants de la pah-treee-eee-ah. . . .*"

His striped toga billowing behind him, O'Dougherty marched into the kitchen. Dora pulled one of the decaying easy chairs away from the table and he stepped into its seat.

"That blood is everywhere!" he shouted. "It reeks from the wafer in your village church. It stinks on the altars of the high places. Bring forth the culprits. Do you remark that senator, his face running with greed, swollen, corpulent with graft? How he whimpers as they hold him up? He has hidden in the dark passages. In the hallways, the committee and cloak rooms, a rat of the passageways. And now, how he blinks as they hold him up to the light. As they bring him out on the white steps. How pale and ghostly, his face. The blue veins tremble in the loose flesh of his cheeks. His belly, how he tries to hide its great girth, as they strip off his suit coat, roll up his shirt sleeves, hoist him to the altar.

"I have seen it!

"I have seen the knife at his throat. I have seen the long, stainless blade, sharp as a razor, laid along that neck. The soft old flesh trying to creep away from the pinprick edge. How the oil of gain streams from the face and the lips wiggle under the gag!"

O'Dougherty's hand slashed the air. "The arteries pour forth. The blood flows out to you. Let it flow in a valley of righteousness, for His namesake. Immerse. Immerse. Let it bathe you. Let it cleanse you. In the great valley of this avenue, I call upon you to dip your hands in the blood. And let us wreak honor, truth, innocence, havoc, terror in this land, no man, no stone, but shall feel . . ."

"Brooklyn Hadassah supports you!"

"Brooklyn Hadassah shall go foremost," cried O'Dougherty. "Brooklyn Hadassah, Hoboken Knights of Columbus, Nashville Lions Club, Tucson Rotary, Kansas City Elks, Los Angeles Red Cross, Idaho Young Democrats, Notre Dame Alumni Association, take your places. March on! March on!"

"Murder!" shrieked Dora as O'Dougherty dismounted the chair and paraded about the room, singing. "Ravish!"

"Rape!"

"In the name of . . ."

"And the . . ."

"*And* the . . ." their voices joined in chorus.

Screaming, they collapsed into each other's arms. Dora felt a hand go under her dress. "Hey! Hey!"

"Hay is for horses," O'Dougherty answered. His hand had crept around her bottom, fingers digging into the plumpness. A knee fell between her legs. The hand was pushing her dress up. She clapped her thighs together, jamming his onslaught, forcing the knee back, holding him off.

"Wwwwwshhhhhhhhhhhhhhh . . ." whistled the teapot in the other room.

"Time out for tea!" sang Dora, breaking away. He lunged to pull her back, but she had slipped across the room. Breathless, O'Dougherty leaned back against the wall. St. Joseph thought the world would melt but, he crooned to himself, panting, liked the way his finger . . . "Where are those papers?" he called.

"In the desk drawer, at the bottom."

"Where?"

"The desk drawer."

O'Dougherty heaved his aching bulk off the wall moving toward the bedroom. A little black desk stood by the window. O'Dougherty grasped the brass knobs of the drawer under a slanting top. He pulled. It was stuck. He thrust forward, pulled back. Shook it from side to side.

"What's the matter?"

"A curse!" He smashed a fist into it, to jar the runners loose.

"Try it gently," Dora mocked.

The drawer rolled out.

Bound with elastic bands in the open box was the packet. A bundle of yellowing magazines, documents, photostats, it glowed. O'Dougherty's hand closed around the package.

Slipped a forefinger under the elastic band, extracting the first document. He recognized the simple, slanting, round-bellied hand, Palmer method. Here and there the clerk had rolled a letter with an extra frill, a double loop on the tail of a letter, enjoying what he was taking down in old plain style.

October 13

Drunk and did abuse his wife, threatening, "Hit her with an axe," said Harold Saw, placed under arrest. Officers Moody and Tuttle. Bail $200.

8:00 P.M.

William Star, age twelve, for alleged molestation of nine-year-old sister. Mrs. Star accompanied him but had to be restrained from attacking boy and generally swearing. The accused, William, was badly bruised. Seen by Doctor Sparks, who said it was all right to put him in cell. Charged with rape of sister, Susan Star, in cornfield back of Star house. Sister came with mother and son but Doctor Sparks sent her home. Father missing for last seven years. Mother threatened to kill him (son), had to be locked up.

William Star
Bail $5,000.
Wilhamena Star
Bail $10.

. . . The boy sitting in the field of ruined corn. The husks silken, empty, like masks in the desolate autumn. Poking with a stick into hulks, battering, chaff under his brutal staff. The wooden pole splintered at the end of its shaft, a cutting edge, tightened into a steel blade in his hand as the tall ghosts before him crashed, hacked, helpless to the ground.

He stood up, the sun gleaming in his eyes, blinded, began to chop a path, withered armies of the field, here, there, a stubborn one, the wind talking through the stalks of anger, terror, resistance, in his path as he parried, cut, hewing them down, clearing a broad way before him, leaving broken countries in his wake. Armies rose up before him. He left strange lands behind among the fallen rows, the spines of their heroes cleft by his blows. He marched forward, kicking the underbrush out of his way, slaughter, relentless, wearying, his arm rising and falling. . . .

He saw her. At the edge of the field, she was watching, blond tassels as white as the threads that had caught in the slivers of his stick. She didn't move. And he turned in her direction and began to cut his way through the dead gray stalks, butchering to his left and right, furiously smashing them, down, down, they came, his blows, magical, severing swiftly, surely, at the base so they toppled at a single slash.

And he hewed into that valley for her. He thrust himself forward, his arm swinging, stalks crashing down on all sides, whipping, stinging, his face burning, crushing thousands, tens of thousands under his heel. Hosts swayed between them as he struck. And she moved among the stalks. And he turned in a circle, flayed them out of the ground, clearing a camp in their midst. Beating on heads, shoulders, backs, until their knees crumpled, cracked. Down to the frozen ground he beat them. Uprooting the stubborn ones among them, mad, blind, furious, as their bodies fell one upon another in heaps below him, snapping underfoot. He stood alone, victorious, under the sky, in a clearing in the midst of the armies.

He was breathing hard, leaning on the stick in the center of his plain, not a figure standing for ten feet around. His arm ached. He didn't have to look. Shivered, the sun was slipping under a cloud. He knew she was there.

He sat down. It was his resting place. Put the stick across his lap, lay back on the couch of stalks, waiting. Holding his breath. Remembering a bird in the dead brush of the marsh, right below him, alive, beating, the silence, fluttering a second, his hands cupping to hold it but it burst as he moved into the sky.

Her eyes met his. The silken hair trembled, silvery in the gray afternoon light. He could see her tiny breasts under the tight red and white jersey, a little boy's shirt, once his. She wore a skirt, though. Her slender legs seemed prettier than any he had ever seen. Her blue eyes wide at the slaughter. She was looking at him. It made him flush, but he fought down the dizzy warmth, gripped the wood in his hand, digging it into the cold earth through the corn bodies.

"Hi," she seemed to say, but it was in a whisper if at all and he stared back to silence her. And slowly she glided toward him in the hush, as he rose she sat down on the husks and he sat down, too, and they stared at each other.

The sun flashed from behind a gray cloud and poured gold all over the rustling couch, her small snub nose and pink lips lighting up with a sudden glow. The warmth in the cool air spreading over his face almost like a mask of heat. He felt the sun like fire spreading through the husks under him. And he held his breath again, letting it out slowly, hearing hers, too, drawn slowly in and out, her body absolutely still but her jersey moving up and down.

He took the pole off his lap and laid it to the side. She leaned forward, putting out her hand, the white forefinger and the nail with a bit of red like a dot touched the stick. She pressed her finger down, pushing the round wood shaft, slowly sat back up, staring at him.

His hand reached out toward her foot. His fingers found the strings of her blue sneakers, tied with a bow. Gently, he tugged at it and the cloth string came sliding out easily. He took off first one of her sneakers, then the other. She said nothing. Looking at him. Her blue eyes curious. And she wiggled her toes now on the rough straw. And she drew her knees up, so that he saw under her skirt of blue denim. He could see green cotton, a little curve of fat that he wanted to touch. And he put his hand between her legs to touch it. And her eyes opened so blue and huge but steady, not wavering. Her skin felt so silken there, like the tassels. She stared as he pulled her panties off and pushed her skirt back and looked at her. She wants to see me, too. And he unhitched the leather belt of his dungarees, the steel pin slipping out of its hole easily, peeling them down to his ankles and the white cotton shorts with them, stepping out of them quickly, throwing them to the side.

They looked at each other. Wondering at the strange excitement he saw now in her eyes. So that she drew the striped red jersey over the tassels of her blond hair. Her breasts were small, but the tips stood up. She was naked. He was naked. And in the whiteness he had to half-rise, crouching over her, bending down to brush her lips. He felt the silk of her limbs. He let himself down upon her, finding a place, his body shivering from her, the wind whistling at their whiteness. Feeling her sink into the soft mattress of the shucks, crunching underneath, her legs spreading apart now, and he fell into a place of such strangeness bathed in tears of wet happiness.

A fear, bitter as ice, gripped him. The sun had disappeared. He looked up.

His mother stood over him, her face frozen in amazement.

His sister began to cry. "He made me."

In terror he gripped the stick, jumped up, ran. Scratched and scored, naked through the rows of stalks, stretching miles, miles. Hearing the scream, the ear-splitting scream

"What are you dreaming about?"

Dora stood over O'Dougherty with a cup of tea.

He waved the torn page at her. "How'd you get it?"

"Why don't you call now?" she asked. "They could come right over to pick up the papers."

"Can we use this?"

Dora took the packet from him. She drew a slip of paper out, an official form.

Dakota County, Iowa

December 13,

By order of the Court of Juvenile Offenders William Star is committed to the Sioux City Psychopathic Hospital on a charge of criminal rape and incest.

"The mother and sister?"

"Both dead."

"So that's all."

Dora laughed. "That's all. That's all. That's all."

O'Dougherty put down his cup of tea. "Come here."

Dora sat down on the edge of the bed. He turned on his side and the toga slumped to his waist. "Let's stay at our respective poles," she cautioned.

"We are poles apart." She was leaning back against the wall. The dress had hiked up on her legs. He could see the little steel buckles of her garter belt. Still on his side, O'Dougherty was close enough to her lap to smell the musk between the tops of her nylons. The elastic band snapped. Dora had taken out a thick document. She handed it to him.

THE STATE OF IOWA
MEDICAL BOARD

Des Moines
Capitol Building
March 5,

This committee was duly constituted and authorized by the Medical Board of the State of Iowa and delegated by said Board to investigate and report on procedures and administration at the Sioux City Psychopathic Hospital, Sioux City, Iowa. Funds allotted under Title A: Medical Administration Act: Passed March 10, 1920: Legislative Acts of the State of Iowa: See Appendix: April 1929: Legislative Acts: Section 18 & 24. Also By-Laws: March 1930: Further references cf. 1905 & 1888: index pg. 1986.

This investigation was undertaken upon receipt of a complaint made to and in cooperation with the acknowledgment and approval of the Commissioner of Health of the State of Iowa and the Board of Hospitals of the State of Iowa. Counsel of the office of the State of Iowa Legislative Subcommittee on Health and Welfare in the State of Iowa has been consulted in the preparation of this report and sections of the Special Report to the Attorney General on the Sioux City Psychopathic Hospital.

A committee of ten was selected. Dr. Mathias Hansen, Dean of the Iowa State Medical School; Dr. Melchador Kozol of the Keokuk College of Pharmacy; Dr. Elie De Voto, Chairman of the Dubuque County Board of Medicine . . .

O'Dougherty's eyes wandered down the dry paragraphs of dusty legislative prose, looking for the dark ink that Dora had promised. He flipped over a page or two crowded with titles and numerals, enabling acts and index numbers. Suddenly his eye arrested:

The Committee arrived at the Sioux City Psychopathic Hospital at nine o'clock on the morning of February 10 and was informed that Doctor Gonzalez and Doctor Gomez were no longer in residence. A meeting with Doctor Emile Borden, resident director of the hospital, and his staff was immediately called. It convened in the South Ward of the building on the third floor. Upon the request of the Committee, hospital records were brought to this room to be examined.

O'Dougherty looked quickly at the two photographs of medical diplomas that had been stapled into the printed report.

Upon a motion of Dr. Kozol, unanimously adopted by the Committee, telegrams were immediately sent to Cristobal University, San Juan, Puerto Rico, asking for confirmation of diplomas awarded to Dr. Raphael Christus Gonzalez and Dr. Fidel Columbus Gomez on June 12, 1932 and June 12, 1933, respectively.

. . . The records show that during the seven months, from July 21 to February 9, that Dr. Raphael Gonzalez and Dr. Fidel Gomez were in residence at the Sioux City Psychopathic Hospital, out of a total patient registration not exceeding 300 during the said period, 147 patients underwent radical surgery under operative techniques introduced by Dr. R. C. Gonzalez and Dr. Fidel F. C. Gomez.

. . . in the month of August, two lobotomies, one partial lobotomy, one "voluntary" castration, one "voluntary" sterilization. There were performed in the month of September four lobotomies, two partial lobotomies, three "voluntary" castrations, one "involuntary" castration and three "voluntary" sterilizations.

. . . so that the records show a total of 75 full lobotomies, 25 partial lobotomies, 20 "voluntary" castrations, five "involuntary" castrations, 12 "voluntary" sterilizations and ten operations of an "exploratory" nature.

It was the testimony of Dr. Emile Borden, that Dr. Gomez and Dr. Gonzalez, after consultation with himself and his staff, had introduced these techniques of radical surgery, stating that such techniques were "the latest innovation in humane and therapeutic treatment of the mentally ill." Dr. Gonzalez and Dr. Gomez, according to Dr. Borden, also stressed the advantages of these techniques to efficient control and handling of patient loads in ward management.

Dr. Borden asked the Committee if this was not so. Dr. Hansen stated that the Committee must refrain from giving answers to such questions; that the Committee had been instructed to act in a purely investigative capacity; that it could not evaluate, either approving or condemning specific surgical methodology; but could merely reiterate the directive of the Iowa State Medical Board, issued on February 8th, which asked for an immediate cessation until further notice of all radical surgery on psychiatric patients, other than that deemed necessary by acute medical emergence.

The Committee, at this point, was interrupted. Western Union advised that there was no address for a School of Medicine attached to Cristobal University in San Juan, Puerto Rico.

Upon unanimous motion of the Committee, the telegram returned was redirected to the Office of the President, Cristobal University. Another was sent to the Medical Board of the Territory of Puerto Rico.

Miss Bernice Lay, R.N., Supervisor of Nursing at the Sioux City Psychopathic Hospital, testified that the radical therapy introduced by the two doctors, Gomez and Gonzalez, had simplified the difficult task of proper patient supervision on the wards. Violent behavior and "acting out" had decreased by 50 percent since the introduction of these surgical techniques, not only among those operated on, who, it was stated, sat quietly in the corners of their wards afterward, but those who had been approached about giving consent to operations had "quieted down considerably." Also, it had become possible to release 22 of the castrates who had been committed as criminally insane and a menace to the community, as no longer posing a significant threat. On cross examination by Dr. De Voto, it was admitted by Miss Lay that the "voluntary" castrates had been told that a condition of their agreement to being operated on would be their release from the hospital. Two of the "involuntary" castrates had also been released, as their behavior, according to the testimony of Miss Lay, and corroborated by a Dr. McCarthy of the hospital, had undergone a "marked change for the good" after the operations.

After a recess of 15 minutes, announced by Dr. Hansen, Chairman of the Committee, Dr. De Voto asked Miss Lay if she knew the average age of the women sterilized. Miss Lay replied that she "was not sure." Dr. Voto stated that upon examination of the records he had discovered that of the 12 women sterilized, three had been above the age of sixty. Dr. De Voto asked if there were any reason to suppose that they were capable of bearing children at that age. Miss Lay stated that the women had been "acting up awfully funny" and Dr. McCarthy corroborated this.

Dr. De Voto, addressing himself to Dr. Charles N. McCarthy of the Sioux City Psychopathic Hospital, asked if Dr. McCarthy could give the Committee any idea of the "exploratory" operations that had been performed on the patients. Dr. McCarthy said that he had only been present at one, and that it was a routine vaginal check. Dr. De Voto asked that the records of the patients who had undergone "exploratory" operations be separated from the files and presented to the Committee for immediate scrutiny. After a recess of ten minutes, called by the Chairman of the Committee, Dr. Hansen, Dr. Voto resumed his questioning, stating that upon examination of the records, he had discovered that the age of every patient upon whom an "exploratory" had been performed was between thirteen and twenty-one, that all ten patients were female, and that the details of the operations as charted were unusually vague. Dr. De Voto asked Dr. McCarthy if it were possible that the "exploratory" the latter had witnessed might have been an abortion. Dr. McCarthy replied in the negative. Miss Lay replied she "was not sure."

The Committee at this point was interrupted. Western Union advised that there was no address for Cristobal University, San Juan, Puerto Rico. The second telegram was from the Medical Board of the Territory of Puerto Rico, San Juan, Puerto Rico. A copy of this telegram will be found in the appendix to the report. It was read aloud to the Committee and to the staff of the Sioux City Psychopathic Hospital on the third floor in the South Ward of the Building.

Dr. Emile Borden rose, after the reading of the second telegram, to offer his resignation. Dr. George Hansen, Chairman of the Committee, stated that the Committee was not empowered to receive resignations and that Dr. Borden would have to submit said resignation to the trustees of the Sioux City Psychopathic Hospital or through other already existing channels; that the Committee had been instructed . . .

O'Dougherty's eyes raced through the paragraphs searching for the name, the name, the name. . . . He found it, a few pages on, at the bottom of a long list of released patients.

. . . William Star: Age eighteen; committed for psychiatric observation after a criminal assault on his younger sister. Released on December 21, 19— by the Sioux City Psychopathic Hospital as rehabilitated after castration.

"Where'd you get to?" Dora broke in.

O'Dougherty looked up from the report at her. She had drawn her legs up to her chin, curling up on the bed, back to the wall. He caught a brief look at silk before her legs flashed together and down. He held the report out, pointing to the page, name.

Dora took it, scanned the remaining pages. She closed the thick pamphlet. "You ready?"

"How did you get on to this?"

"Back files. We had a whole floor with nothing but stacks of old detective pulp. It was a graveyard. Occasionally someone would dig up a dead story, resurrect it as a curiosity item. You know, Lizzy Borden, the Kansas Strangler of 1910. Put a little zippy prose on the bones, it's as good as new. I used to read them in the office, especially when I first went to work there, trying to pick up the style of the dirt columns. It's a craft, O'Dougherty. You have to have a feeling for exploitation writing. Here . . ."

She dropped the pamphlet. Her long fingers reached into the packet on the bed and extracted an old magazine. Its pages were yellow. The cheap pulp was already crumbling along the edges, saw toothed, malevolent. Folded open in the center, one page was a collage of photographs, the other screamed:

(too awful to tell)

IOWA'S HORROR HOSPITAL

When two Spanish Surgeons wielded the scalpel like a scalping knife and left a trail of bleeding genitals behind!

Somewhere in the sands of a great American desert along a lonely stretch of road, a young man walked slowly and painfully. His face is distorted like an animal's. The birds caw and shriek about his head. He howls back. A few weeks before, he was released from the Sioux City Psychopathic, where a team of mad doctors castrated him. He and 40 others were set free from the hospital after being subjected to horror operations in which their sexual organs were removed. *They were the lucky ones!*

On February 10, 19–, a shocked committee of doctors in a dingy ward of the Sioux City Psychopathic Hospital, holding special hearings at the request of the State Medical Board, heard of a series of fantastic operations performed by two natives of Puerto Rico who had posed as doctors.

Bristling with diplomas and newly minted medical certificates, Raphael Gonzalez and Fidel Gomez bustled up to the front door of the Sioux City Psychopathic one sunny July day and were promptly hired by its credulous director. For a week or two, the pseudo-doctors behaved themselves, contented with cutting cuticles and fingernails. But hospital routine turned dull, so the volatile Latins decided to do a bit of fancy slicing and asked the director and his staff for permission to show off their skill with cutlery. Just a lobotomy or two—to show what we can do?

Before the investigating committee, Dr. Emile Borden, the Director, pleaded in defense that there were too many patients in the hospital and that controlling them was becoming "an awful problem." Drs. Gomez and Gonzalez had come up with a solution for the harried Doctor Borden, turn his charges into helpless vegetables by cutting out the troublesome sections of their brains —lobotomy!

After carving out the root of the problem, the mentally ill could be dumped quietly in the corner where they wouldn't hurt a flea. Nope, no more screams or shouting at Sioux City Psychopathic. Just a heap of vegetables rotting by the wall that the nurses could wheel between meals and bedtime.

When the first two or three operations in August ran true to form, yielding a fine crop of cabbages, an enthusiastic Dr. Borden turned over half his patients to the wild Puerto Ricans, who chopped out over a hundred brains in their six-month stay. But the Latin doctors were itchy in other parts beside their fingers. The Committee report lists several "exploratory" operations that were rumored to be abortions, especially as they were performed on young and pretty female patients.

Ugliest of all the surgery practiced by these two merry young internes was the castration and sterilization of three dozen of the mentally ill. Persuading the pliant Dr. Borden that criminal sexual desire could be cut out of a human being, Dr. Gonzalez and Dr. Gomez began to flick the knife among the private parts of patients with a record of sexual aberration. By promising to set them free afterward, the hot-blooded doctors were able to gain the consent of many of their victims, but even without it, they snipped and sawed.

Soon frightened parents and relatives were besieging the State Medical Board with questions. An inquiry was ordered and the Spanish doctors skipped away the day before the official investigating committee arrived. Suprisingly, they left a good impression behind them at the hospital. The head of nursing, Miss Bernice Lay, R.N., testified that they were "personable young men." And one of the staff, a Dr. McCarthy, stated that he believed them "competent and hardworking young physicians. A credit to their profession."

Imagine the surprise of the hospital, then, when it turned out that Gonzalez and Gomez were no doctors at all but a couple of medical students who had been thrown out of school in Miami for "aberrant sexual behavior." What a switch! An eight-state alarm went out for the bogus physicians, but the police two years later have yet to catch up with them.

And what about the patients, castrated or sterilized, who were set free? Some have been locked away again. Others are still at large. They have assaulted children and adults before. Is the desire for unmentionable sexual acts really gone? Or will they strike next in your backyard?

O'Dougherty put the magazine down on the bed.

"Do you blame him?" she asked.

"Who?"

"William Star."

"I don't know."

"Are you afraid?"

O'Dougherty shifted in his bright toga.

"Shall we take a trip to sunny California?" Dora asked, leaning forward. He could see her full breasts swelling the frills of a white shirt front. The woolen jacket of her suit was unbuttoned, open. O'Dougherty felt a cold wind blow in the window. He shivered in the bath towel. "Whoever banged out that article headed him in the right direction," she continued, not waiting for a reply.

"The blind guesser . . ." he mumbled.

"He took the Southern route. Hitching rides and walking through the picturesque Southwest. Shall we join him as he floats by raft down to Kansas City; shall we walk by his side as he strides through the shadows of reeling gunmen in the streets of Dodge City; shall we cross the old Cimarron with him into the dry, dusty Texas Panhandle; walk, our face black with sun, into Sante Fe and on through painted deserts and petrified forests, pennies in his pocket, crazy between his legs, and running, running, putting distance between him and the state of Iowa, leaving mountains, hills, sands, valleys behind him until . . ."

"The Pacific, beautiful, boundless, sparkling, rolling out to the vast calm. A young man plunges into the joyous, lilting surf, washes his aching limb. And then on, to the magic heap of clay, the wicked, sprawling city of Los Angeles, where the hero loses himself among the host of strange angels, among hairy motorcycle cops, cultists, movie stars, senior citizens, palm-strewn boulevards, alleys, perpetual sun, warmth, smog, filth, fornication."

Dora's brown eyes shone black, polished jewels. "Thrown into the hot humus of Southern California, our friend blooms in lush, vivid colors. Out of the mutilated bulb springs exotic, erotic flowers. Smell!"

She snatched up a carbon from the bundle and threw it at O'Dougherty. It was on the stationery of the magazine she had worked for.

(*The story that the cops tried to hush*)

QUEEREST PATRIOT OF ALL

Did the Commander
put on *lipstick*
for his troops?

No one knew it, but the April ball of the "queens" of Los Angeles was harboring a distinguished guest when the cops burst in to break up the gathering of West Coast fairies. Because when one of the Cinderellas they dragged into the tank, sporting a blond wig, high-heeled pumps, pierced ears, and a floor-length gown of satin with shimmering sequins, screaming obscenities, was stripped to her red nylon panties, the tender fingers of the vice squad were stayed by the embarrassing disclosure that they had superpatriot William Star, Commander of the California Continentals, in drag.

No sooner was it whispered in the ear of the unbelieving sergeant at the station than the rough, unfriendly paws of his lions were restrained, a golden coach, the Commander's Lincoln Continental limousine, pulled up and Cindy Star was whisked off into the night.

Lean, lantern-jawed, the fearless Commander stood the very next day in a Sacramento football stadium. He pledged that in case of a sneak attack or any other looming terror, the Continentals would prevent "ass kissers" from surrendering the country. Moral shock troops would man the mountain passes. Ten thousand Continentals shouted and cheered. Commander Star's manly chest swelled under the black uniform with patriotism. No one knew he was wearing a bra.

There were two or three sheets more of the carbon, but O'Dougherty looked up abruptly. "Who wrote this?"

"Me!"

He looked at her. Dora raised her legs. He could see her snaps again.

"Why wasn't it printed?"

"It was too dirty. The mug shots had been removed from the police station. Fingerprints, too. I had a copy of the record, but you stir up a hornet's nest if something compromises the cops. It was wrong for our readership, Continental types, half would cancel subscriptions. There would be pressure, big, ugly, the Continentals would have bought us off. It would never get past our printers."

"I don't believe you."

"Right. I never submitted it."

"Why?"

"It was a lie."

"The facts?"

"No, the way I wrote it. None of the cops knew who the blond queer was. She made her call to an attorney. Fifteen minutes later the phone was ringing from City Hall. Release her. Tear up any shots or records of the arrest. Even when they took the wig off, nobody recognized her. They had gotten past her panties. They found out she had no balls and called the sergeant in. She was crying. He sent the other cops out of the room and began to ask questions. He found he had William Star on his hands. Then the phone call came and they hustled her out. The sergeant took the mug shots and fingerprints to drop them in the basket, but . . ."

Dora paused, smiling. Her mouth puckered. "I paid him a hundred bucks for the documents." She looked at O'Dougherty, waiting for his eyes to come up from her snaps. "He was a member—a Continental."

She felt her dress shift over the buckles, an inch or two, as she brought her legs up, leaning back, she spoke softly.

"There was a stink and a smell in the little room back of the sheriff's office in Los Angeles: the puke of drunks and the odor of warm piss. They had just ripped the blond wig off the queer they hauled in out of the sheriff's station wagon, and big, vicious marshals with faces like bulldogs were going to town. She screamed as they pulled off her nylons and crammed them in her mouth. Screamed. Choked. A long skinny nightstick waved in the air before her. It rapped across her mouth so that she tasted pink lipstick like peppermint, the sour blood of her gums, and pain shooting up, nauseous. And they pushed her down on the floor, the nylons gagging in her mouth with blood. Two hairy cops sweating and laughing took hold of her legs. The polished nightstick smashed her mouth again, waved by a grinning face. Then she felt something between her legs, rammed, twisted, so that she rose squirming as they pushed her down on the cold, wet concrete, banging her head to keep her quiet.

"It was pulled out; they stuck the end of it in her nose, dangled it before her, whacked her mouth again. She tried to stand up. They pushed her down, shoved it in again, bunching her red underwear, the pain screaming up, so that she banging with her fists on the cement, had to be sat on. And the pimply face, oozing drool and laughter, made a fist, kept making a fist before her eyes, then reached into the nylon panties. . . ."

Silence in the room. Dora's eyes shone with the reflected light of a naked bulb, electricity circling, arcing through the room. "Come on, boy." She slumped against the wall, pulling her dress down to her crotch, picking it up to her belly button. Her fingers slashed her panties off. She wiggled them down to her knees.

O'Dougherty was paralyzed on the bed, shattered. Pain held him limp, helpless before her.

"Oooooo."

Dora's eyes were ferocious, in flame. He stared at her nakedness. "Are you going to?"

O'Dougherty stirred in the bath towel. "Turn him in!" she screamed. The alarm went off, out of nowhere, the air bursting into a thousand fragments. "Too late!" she shrieked, jumping up, pulling herself together. Dora ran into the kitchen, snatching her purse off the back of a chair. "Get dressed. I'll wait. In the hallway."

The door slammed behind her.

Down, down, deep in the subways toward New Jersey, Dora and O'Dougherty pushed off, shoved into the channels of their dreams, along flashing steel rails, sun spots of electric light, shadows of passageways, hurtling headlong, they dreamed and were driven.

She strained, the bench chattering under her as if loose, and the shiver of the whole train ran through her, racing from afternoon to afternoon, one spinning out of the wheel, the spokes a blank disk, gray, white, blinding, the counters of her father's store; and she was trapped on an afternoon in the four-o'clock lull standing alone in the lingerie. Age sixteen, her black hair short, a schoolgirl's skirt, plaid wool cut to just below her knees, white socks, scuffed loafers. Her ass pressed into a wooden counter rim; hearing a hot rod accelerating, roaring in the street, a black Buick convertible, four duck-tailed young men who rode the thoroughfare, searching; she dreamed of white Cadillac limousines, drugstore hoodlums turned doctors, lawyers, accountants, respectable husbands, million-dollar homes, maids, swimming pools.

Dora tried to hold that moment against the rim of the girdle counter. That last instant but slowly she could not help recall the tingling in her leg, the itchiness of her ass, her irritation at the hours among the cotton towers of ladies' goods, and slowly the growing sensation that she, too, had a right to the toilet, where her father had sat for two hours, perched in study of holy books, his pants down. "I have to go, too!" she whispered, furiously, silently. And pushed off the wooden rim of the counter on tiptoe stealthily with muffled footsteps to the back of the store.

There, behind a musty curtain, the door no one approached unasked. Not even her mother. "Get away! Get away!" Near hysteria whenever footsteps came. "Away! Away!"

Yet she came; two hours she had spent standing alone, waiting on customers, her father's favorite; on toward the door along the cracked yellow linoleum though Dora wished herself back, she silently pushed aside the dusty, heavy cloth, her nose against the door, about to knock.

The girl's hand stopped in the air. Was he really taking a . . . Despite the insistence of her need, some delicacy stirred. Girlishly, she bent to . . . Dora could not help it. Slowly, stooped, looked through the keyhole, odd-shaped opening, into the toilet stall's dim interior.

And everything stopped. Though Dora was desperate to fall back, back from the keyhole, back among the counters, back in time, childhood; the young girl's eye at the keyhole, seeing, having to look and look, make sense of, no sense of, needing to register that figure seated in the gray light of the stall. A minute, she knelt, not drawing breath, then rose, listening to every creak in the floor, every snap, each crack of her joints, stepping back into the counters, the crashing neon above.

O'Dougherty started up from his thoughts, lean flanks rattling in the plastic hollows.

Two red eyes regarded him balefully. A face bristling with soft gray whiskers, thrown back against the window of the subway, jittering as if the train were the agent of delirium tremens.

A pink bone showed through a hole in the knee. A spot of blood spread like Cancer, the crab, on the shirt front, a rag knotted at the neck.

In a sudden jar of the train the man lurched toward him, alcohol reeling across the aisle, unsweetened through the press, the whiskey gone bad on the breath, a cesspool. O'Dougherty's belly turned, rolling with the jumping, jolting car.

Red, red before his eyes. The face burning in the chair beside the grate of coals, broken bottles scattered over the deep Oriental rugs. John O'Dougherty seated in his father's chair, the stuffing beginning to show through the fraying green threads, shouting filthy words, his wife and daughters huddled in the bedroom out of range of the bottles hurled at the pretty knicknacks of the room. A bottle shattered the window and splintered glass onto the sidewalk, bringing a swarm of blue coats up the stairs, brushing by the boy in the doorway, into the room, to take him by force out of the chair, blood running down the cheek of one from a cut over the eye. "Jesus, he's a tough son of a bitch, even stinko."

"Oh, it's a sad day," murmured the elderly one with the stripes on his shoulder, "a sad day for the family." They carried the struggling, cursing body, four of them, big, brawny men twisting his arms as gently as they could behind his back, one of them giving him a quick rap on the head with a nightstick. "Watch it Jimmy! Don't be too rough! Don't be too rough! Into the bedroom when you've shut him up." And bending down to the boy, "Whatever they say, your father's a great man. You believe it."

No, not that red, when his father lay tied down in the bed, mother stretched over him crying, his sisters in the corner, the policemen trotting out, respectfully tipping their hats.

Darker, purple, fear, shame too terrible. Blood flooded O'Dougherty's eyes, not tears, the smell of stale alcohol still in his nose, saw before him that face, haggard, pathetic. Coming in when the rest of the family was out, the boy was quiet on the steps, hearing the strange sounds from the bedroom. Sniffing the whiskey in the flat and walking with the silent tread that was instinct by now when the old man raided the shelves of the store downstairs and began to steam himself in his chair. Which was empty as the boy peeked in from the doorway. And the sounds from the bedroom. He made his way silent as an Indian toward them. Looked in. And could not look away.

Why? Why did he have to stand there? Standing like wood, knowing that sooner or later the face would look up and meet his eyes.

That face staring up from the bed like an animal, the crumpled sheets where his sister, the daughter, lay, her legs spread apart as she had done for him before. And in that naked, hairy body he saw something too naked, like Ham, his father, drunken and secret, and could not move

Until the girl begins to whimper, "Don't tell, don't tell. . . ." Only who can you? as he glides away from the door. No box of confession will receive it, no church that will not turn into hell about him at the first whisper. No, it must burn day after day in the silences between father and son, before he flees the house at last. And again that face flamed in him anew the knowledge of the white legs, varicose-veined, the aged buttocks, his sister's smooth, freckled thighs, sandy tufts of hair and the revealed thing of himself, extended long, limp, ashamed before its own seed. The blood rose in O'Dougherty's eyes and now he almost screamed. The drunk coming forward, his face grizzled, stinking, "Help me. . . ." O'Dougherty pushed him back, in horror, so the man sprawled against the opposite bench and crashed to the rolling floor.

In the empty seat Dora saw a little man with hunched shoulders rock back and forth, the tattered leather-backed book of the Law had slipped to the ground at his feet. His eyes were closed and he crooned to himself, arms crossed over his naked breasts cupped in a pink lace ladies' brassiere. His own underwear lay in a heap on the open pages of the Law, an extravagant cotton marker. And in place of his shorts, a black girdle with nylons hooked into place stretched silently as he bowed in his strange rhythm back and forth. The girl's eyes widened as she stared at the skinny, knobby legs enclosed in sheer hosiery; the flat masculine tits encircled in a small brassiere; but especially at the face, the queer little half-smile, a bit crooked on the lips that twisted and turned in some inner possession. "I see! I see!" she wanted to . . . Only she began to ease back, away from the hole she was staring into, still seeing in the faint light white threads of the brassiere.

"Dora," he said. She jumped, startled. The train jerked and O'Dougherty lunged, collided with the girl. They clung to one another, he grabbed for a strap and held her swaying, then she too, seeing where she was, reached up to secure herself as he bent down over the drunk he had knocked senseless.

Her finger found the hole of the dial. Liberal newspaper. Public service, not scandal. The first digit click click clicked back into place like a miniature guillotine sliding down. She gripped the black stick of the receiver and the bleeding rectum, the nightstick, her father's face, screamed through the mouth. Dora's finger found the hole again, but her hand was shaking. Her finger dragged the blackened circle up along its axis. Dora! Dora! Her hand shaking in the hole, everything before her fell apart. A tremor ran through her, jerking her body as if she were shivering into pieces. I see! I see! Grasping the receiving dumbbell, she brought it down like a club on the phone box. She smashed it like a brute animal and when it fell to the floor, ringing in pain, she kicked, kicked it, slashed it with her hard, sword-sharp heels.

O God! O'Dougherty groaned, blood streaming between his fingers. The floor buckling. Ready to puke. The orifice pouring crimson mucus over the bristles. The subway hurtling itself down along its walls. Out cold, the poor bastard. He held the grizzled face between his hands. Faint from the smell of liquor and gore. Pray for us now and at the hour of our resurrection. Kneeling on the dirt of the shaky floor. I commit this soul into your hands. A sharp, metallic pain stabbed in his belly. What was he doing? Where was he going? Acid came up in his throat as if the bag of his stomach were slit. How could he go out and watch? He, too, wanted a miracle. He, too, wanted to be reborn, shriven, set free. The dossier that rested back on the subway seat—what did it have to do with the possibilities of this night? The rails throbbed beneath him. The priest might be vile and still handle the body of Christ. The Messiah himself might bear taint and yet ascend. He came like Judas to betray.

Drums beat on the subway track. The iron clangor of the wheels. His head rang, deep barrels, goatskins, thunder out of that late afternoon high in the Adirondacks.

Sporting a black cap and uniform borrowed from a tailor in the city, he had gotten off the bus after a headache-ridden eight-hour drive. Thousands of cars tooted their horns; the caps of hundreds of posts swarming in the field outside the little village, among the bright brass patches of the bands gathered for the initiation. O'Dougherty saluted everyone in sight, nervous. His hand kept going down to his crotch, scratching. It itched like mad. His uniform was crumpled and sweaty. The long, cramped bus ride in the middle of the summer had unsettled him and the shouting and boisterous drumming ached in the hollows of his eyes.

A hairy, two-fingered hand had reached out for him as he stepped off the bus. It grabbed his own in a grip that cracked bones. "Hi, young feller, where you from?"

"New York City. . . ."

"Y' come a long way. Good fer you. Y'll find a lot o'y' boys over *that* way."

The crippled hand of the tall, gaunt Continental, an Official Greeter with medals down to his belly button, pushed him good-naturedly to the left in the crowd. O'Dougherty walked a few yards in that direction, looked around to assure himself that the Greeter was busy with another, then turned and walked rapidly to the right. Lost now in a mob of beer-reeking men, he pushed toward the grandstand, where Continentals were packed in horseshoe shape up to the sky. Thousands were standing in the open end of the lucky formation. The Ceremony of Innocence must be over, he thought, as he elbowed through the black press of uniforms, for he could see in the corridor staked off with ropes among the mass of rowdy males, girls trekking in groups of four or five out of the stadium. Their communion dresses brilliant white in the corridor of dark jackets. The drums treading a pleasant calypso to their exit. Medically certified fifteen-year-old girls, guaranteed intact. O'Dougherty struggled along the edge of the corridor, trying to make his way through the mob into the wooden stadium. And the pink faces and blond curls, combed down over their backs, came toward him. A group of girls was being escorted out by a suntanned Continental honor guard. Their dresses were more like skimpy nightgowns. The silk clung to the adolescent breasts and buttocks, damp and almost shiny in the heat. You could see through. Men swayed forward on the ropes.

O'Dougherty breathed hard. He began to fight his way harder through the crowd, shaking off the dizzying fumes of sun, headache and whiskey. Reaching the edge of the grandstands, he started to climb. Down in the field one last group of girls was circling a tall, black pole. The spar was hung with pink and blue crepe. It rose from the center of a pungent bed of blooms, for as the girls skipped about it, they threw blossoms at the massive timber from their armfuls of flowers. One by one they danced to the pole, bent forward, and kissed it. Loud roars of approval went up from the stands.

Suddenly there was a blare of trumpets. Breaking off their kissing, the girls assembled in a formation and were marched off the field. The trumpets blared again.

Now people in the stands began to get up and head for the exits. Puzzled, O'Dougherty kept his seat. The jam at the open end of the horseshoe was enormous. He watched the corridor held open for the girls collapse and swallow up their white dresses in screams and shouts. The beat of the calypso grew more intense. Something was waved above the bobbing heads.

Looking about, the stands had thinned considerably. Only a few hundred people were left. O'Dougherty leaned forward. His view of the crowd struggling at the exit was cut off as slowly a black curtain was dragged across the open end of the horseshoe, shutting out the field from the eyes of anyone not in the stands. A finger tapped him.

It dug, a scalpel probing, into his neck. Turning round, he recognized the two-jointed hand. The tall man stared down.

"Y'in the inner S?"

O'Dougherty nodded in the affirmative. He began, however, to burn between the legs.

"Y'got a card?"

"Left it . . . at home . . ." he faltered, shifting in his seat.

"Know the sign?"

"Uh . . ." O'Dougherty's hand scratched nervously at his crotch.

"Right!" said the Continental, beaming. And giving O'Dougherty a snappy scratch, sauntered along his way.

Alone on the grandstand bench, O'Dougherty wiped his brow. Inner S? The trumpets began to sound a slow, mournful dirge. Through a slit in the black cloth, a bull appeared, dark as the curtain but wound about with white streamers.

"You people want to settle y'self down by the ring here?" a voice announced over the loudspeakers. All through the grandstands Continentals stood up and began to move down toward the edge of the field. O'Dougherty, not wishing to seem conspicuous, rose too and descended the shaky wooden steps. He joined the thin line of men hanging on the swaying ropes that cordoned off the bottom of the grandstands from the trodden area where the girls had danced. He saw on the grim, set faces around him that the ceremony had begun.

"I would like to call your attention to the beautiful black Angus bull, specially fattened for this afternoon."

The bull trotted forward into the field. It was huge, even for the breed. "Toppin' the scales at *three thousand* pounds." The oiled darkness of it shimmered in streaks of the afternoon sun. Restless, the beast shook its head and looked around the stadium with unblinking eyes. The line of men swaying on the fragile barriers watched the power of that bulk, breathing. It trotted under the burning sun of the afternoon, trailing ropes.

Two long cords had been belted around its midriff in a harness. They bumped helplessly along the ground as he charged, turned and twisted in a gallop. The men stirred uneasily along the flimsy loops of the barrier.

"Look at him toss his heels! Ain't he a fine fellow?"

A ragged laughter went around the ring from one side of a mouth to another. "Ain't he a beautiful male? My, look at that big rump. And those balls!"

The laughter increased. "A real *A*-ristocrat. Thirteen years old. That old man out there is Father Apis. Look at those lines. A touch of the Brahmin. That old bull has thrown hundreds in his time. And there's plenty more in the sag of those bags."

The bull stopped abruptly in his gallop about the ring. He began to paw the ground, kicking the gravel, sniffing, suspicious.

Soothing, the voice over the loudspeaker squeaked, "What's the matter, Father Apis? Don't mind us talkin' 'bout you, do yuh? I was just telling the folks 'bout your harem. Yes, sir! Those beautiful young creatures. Full tits and fine behinds. How many girls have spread their re-ars for you, y'old dong? All over our state you've squatted mmmmmmmm! Rubbed your balls on white, dark and speckled."

The voice, lewd and knowing, seemed to excite the old bull because his member came thrusting out of its hairy pocket. It jerked down bigger and bigger. The crowd murmured.

"That's right, Apis. Show it to us! I bet it hurts. We have a sweet little Guernsey hot as a tub of liquid butter, just waitin' for it. Get it out into the air. Pharaoh of Egypt called himself *a mighty bull*. See why?"

The black bull reared up, a mass of black gargantuan flesh underscored by a long pink rod.

"How's he look, boys? Ain't he a fine old daddy? Ain't he the sign and symbol of prosperity? Now, you know the rules. Look at him stretch! I want you to *consecrate* old Apis to the *summum bonum. Ad astra. In hoc signo vinces*. Know what it means? *Hallalooh!* Say it again!"

"Hallalooh!" went up in a general shout around the ring.

"Who is gonna throw the first stone?"

A single gold beer can sailed out of the empty grandstands,

sparkled for a second, a star, falling, hit the bull's rear. The can rattled to the ground, the animal hardly acknowledging it. But at the sound of it striking the gravel, hundreds of missiles darkened the air. Stones, bottles, cans, knives, rained down on the shape in the midst of the stadium. Alarmed, the beast lowered its head, trying to locate the source of this painful shower. It snorted and began to move in a circle, stamping the ground.

"There he goes, boys. There he goes!" squawked the voice. "He's mad. He's gonna tear you up. He's gonna kick your balls in. He's big. He's powerful. He can kick shit out of *you* any time he wants!"

In answer, the hail of hard objects redoubled on the angry, thrashing bull. Furious, the animal paused in its circle, then charged to the right. "Get him, boys! Ya-ha-la-looh! Hooh! Hooh!"

O'Dougherty's heart came up in his throat as flesh. In a murderous clatter of hooves the bull rushed toward him, gouging the earth in its frenzy. A crowd of men shouting behind it, urged the massive engine on, screaming, hooting, while the drums exploded in a cacophony over the loudspeakers. The thin line of men around him did not move. They stood fixed and stiff, hardly swaying on the rope barriers. His heart leaped and ran skipping, breaking out of his throat. He felt it pounding up the grandstands. Yet terrified of breaking the grim, unmoving concentration, he stiffened his grip on the hemp barrier as the bull's hooves threw dirt on him, the smell of it charging up into his nostrils, rank, sweet, foul. It loomed over him, the rock hooves rising against the bright sky, higher and higher, the brutal, thick legs shearing the air, so close he felt their wind, saw the pink flesh under the jet belly. Higher and higher it rose to trample him. Rearing back on its hind legs like a battle statue, against the sky, black, blotting out the sun, a second the beast swayed.

O'Dougherty's eyes wide, glazing blind white, incredulous, saw the bull topple back, twisting, crash to the side.

"Yahooh! Yahooh! Hooh! Haa-laa-loooh!" Around him, tense faces breaking into smiles, the stiffened lips shattered into shouting. O'Dougherty was caught up in it. And he charged forward with the rest. The bull, rising again, was running in the opposite direction toward the men who had dragged it down with their end of the rope. Among the pushing, jostling crowd, O'Dougherty, screaming, found himself carried along. Suddenly they stooped, he stooping too, his hand grabbing at a snaking, dirt-stained piece of hemp. He clutched at it and was pulled along by the thrust of the engine at its end. "Pull, you bastards!" someone cried. "Dig in! Dig in!" O'Dougherty jabbed his heels in the dust to brake himself. The dust sprayed into his nose, filled up his shoes. And still he and the others, before and behind him, were dragged, dragged, the line like fire in his hands, dragged, dragged, until he saw, slowly, inch by inch, a black shape, rising, rising against the sky.

"You got him! You got him!" shrieked the loudspeakers, as with a shudder the bull toppled over again and the fiery line went slack.

"Now, don't you let him git!" The line was pulled tight again. The dazed beast jerked onto its feet by the curious harness. Half-human, half-animal, the huge bull was dragged back standing upright on its hind legs. The creature flailing the air with its hooves, protesting, snorting. One of the myrmidons, O'Dougherty tugged on the coarse hemp, dragging the bulk of the black bull back, back, back against the tall pole, the hump of the animal's spine thudding into place. And now the two groups of men began to run clockwise and counterclockwise around the spar so that the moiling animal was trussed tighter and tighter against it. "Bind him! Bind that big bugger! Bind him for a sweet savor."

The bulging barrel of its body belted against the wooden pole, the bull bellowed and frothed at the mouth, foam dripping in ghostly, waving trails from its full, red lips. Its massive head, free of the ropes, battered wildly against the thick post. More than wrath showed in the rolling white eyes. Terror at the unnatural position made the giant frame shake desperately to break loose its bonds. Under the glossy black coat its muscles coiled and uncoiled in knots as it strove to burst free of the outrageous stance, twisting under the abrasive cords. The heat of its breath roared out among the men who had crowded right up next to the animal now that its powerful, chopping forelegs were helplessly pinioned against its body. The beast shook like a colossus on the cruel stake.

A figure dressed in a spotless white sheet was pressing through the mob of black uniforms, which fell back respectfully on each side of him. "Trussed and tied," the loudspeakers announced. "Ain't he!" O'Dougherty was close to the bull. He could smell the odor of the animal again. And reach out to touch its coat running with sweat. Inky drops congealed on the writhing, oily hide.

"How're you, Daddy Apis? You ready? You a little frightened? Come on now, Dad. You've had your fun. Look at those velvet balls."

The man's face was hooded. Two fingers reached out to touch the bull. "My, my, must weigh a ton!" The bull's pink sceptre stood bolt upright. Its eyes clouded purple, as the hand grasped the end of it. A knife flashed in the palm of the man.

O'Dougherty screamed. Agony shot through his groin. He doubled over, ablaze. "Stop! Stop!" he shouted. A heel like a thin, black stiletto had come stabbing down into his crotch. His eyes teared as he grabbed the smooth leg.

"Daddy! Daddy!" screamed Dora. O'Dougherty hugged her leg as the train sliced along the long blades of the subway tracks.

Outside, the dazzling neon crackled in green, blue, red, streaking the room with the rainbow of its letters—"NEW." It hissed "NEW" through faulty circuits that had extinguished the bottom of the sign.

Dole was folded over in the closet. Ark had knocked him out with pills, force-fed. Manageable, momentarily sleepy, wrists bound to his ankles, the priest was stuffed among coats, black jackets, dresses, wedged tight into a thicket of wire and wooden triangles, his purple nose just touching the carpet dust.

They were up high, the thirtieth floor, a long drop from the bedroom window of the hotel to the street, or the alley below the airshaft of the bathroom.

Billy Jim was in there giving Star a bath, laying on the hands, again and again, soaping him up and down, trying to calm the guy, give him back the spirit, get him ready for the night.

Paul faced Ark in the bedroom. They were seated on opposite sections of the twin-bed set, the telephone between them.

He wanted to call, but Ark caught his wrist. "Take a nap."

Gogarty shifted on the bed. He ached. He shoulda known better. Didn't have the balls to push the guy aside, get up and find out what was goin' on . . . gone . . . the last few weeks . . . everything. It was his goon squad in the next room, a bunch of good guys, bookies, toughs from Eastie, yet he . . .

Shit, his head was fuzzy.

That knock on the head? Or the beer . . . Star wouldn't touch . . . green bubbles rose in the bathtub around the slim body. It sprang up, danced out the door, around the room, onto the beds, tumbling, fell back with him, shiny sequins, jingling, legs, red-hot momma, whoo hoooh . . . a red glow overspread Ark's features.

Gogarty felt the wet sheets where his palms rested on the edge of the bed. He smelled the fume of beer coming up from the mattress. His pants were unzipped.

Star was in the bathroom. Shit, he needed a shower. They had locked the door. You could hear the moaning and splashing, the soap bar gripped in two fingers, laving the body; Billy Jim in the bathtub, bending over with dripping pants.

I need a priest. I gotta talk to someone, thought Gogarty. I'm dopey. He felt the black slate floor, damp and slick, the fat of his ass slapping as he slipped back against the wall, giggling. His brother's little thing stood up like a candle ". . . ooooh gimmee, gimmee. . . ." Their bathing trunks hung in the locker room. The sand in his crotch tickled, made the curly hair tingle as he rubbed the soap bar, its creamy lather round and round, "C'mon, c'mon. . . ." The bubbles stung his tip, but it felt so crazy, he couldn't stop, his body heaving, "Hey . . ." he said, "you know what . . . let's . . ."

The phone rang. Ark picked it up, laughed, hung up. "Wrong number," he said, raising his eyebrows.

Jesus, just to go and sprinkle a little water on his face.

He should get up, go around and check everything out. Tonight was over with already. Tomorrow was the big day.

Next week they were gonna announce. He had almost enough delegates lined up in one party and the other had a handful of shmucks no one cared about, running. There was a file on every county chairman, every state committeeman, with enough filth to choke them to death, stink them out of politics. There would be no way to stop the nomination.

If they wanted one. They were still debating whether or not to run him as an Independent. America was sick of both parties. There was nothing but a bunch of mediocrities on either side.

They were supposed to get the files out, boxes of them in the next room, and go over the names. A lot of chicken shit had to be shaken up. People who didn't like this country were gonna get a one-way ticket out. Fuckin' profs and bankers, sneerin' at him? Right in the ear!

Gogarty shook his head. It was too hot in the room. He was sleepy. "How 'bout . . ." He couldn't finish. I gotta wake up. He had scores to settle.

He was gonna go after those wise guys in the middle. The boys would go home tomorrow and start pushin' 'em out, fuckin' two-facers, their hands in the till, talkin' like they were better than anyone. No balls.

The walls ran green again. Gogarty suddenly felt sick, as if he'd been kicked in the groin. His ass ached.

He wanted a priest. What's the matter? he thought. I'm dopey. Oh shit, come on, he growled to himself. I'm just confused, see, that's all, too many beers. Get Dole out of the closet, he'll do. How'd he get in there?

He couldn't remember. Zip up your pants, come on, move!

"Hey," he said to Ark. "How 'bout some coffee?"

"Keep you up."

"C'mon . . ."

He was turning over on his tummy, dripping bubbles. Sliding, he put his hand behind him and pulled the little candle to his crack, then pushing apart the buns of flesh, tasted periwinkle, salt of the beach outside, pine deodorant, sweat of male bathers, scum along the groove of the drainpipe, "C'mon . . . do it," he whispered, "do it. . . ."

"Hey!"

Stiff, two dogs, all fours, they froze.

"Hey!"

He didn't dare look up but waited until something tore him off and slammed into the stall slate, blood ran out his nose, soap.

A bronze foot swung down and caught him in the stomach, "Fuckin' blubber!"

Sick, he couldn't run . . . sprawling, trying to rise, the trunks slapped in his face.

"Put 'em on!"

He stumbled, was dragged out past the white-haired manager, the attendants all shaking their heads, he could hardly see through his tears, pushed into the office, crying, shaking.

"What's your name?" The voice that had struck at him in the shower. He looked up at the man, dressed now, a cop.

"His name is Gogarty. . . ." The attendants knew him, his brother.

"Where's the little one?"

"He got away."

"Where's he live?"

"Over by Peter and Paul's—in the shanties."

"Hey!"

He couldn't help . . . it stung in his pants, down the bare calf into his shoe.

"Shit, smell it."

He stood shivering in his cut-off corduroys and sockless shoes.

"Little piss pot!" The tanned hand caught his elbow, shook it so hard he spattered on the floor. "Give him some pants." They threw a pair of paint-spotted dungarees at him and he climbed into the oversize trouser legs, tripped as the arm pushed him forward, out of the bathhouse. Dragged onto the beach, then to the sidewalk, shaken, the fat of his arm was pinched between sharp fingernails.

"You fuckin' little frigger. . . ." They turned at a street corner and he got a slap in the face, pushed away a second later as he started to smell again.

"What *are* you, a fuckin' girl?" His hair was grabbed, yanked through the streets of Southie, everyone looking at him, his nose running over his face, he couldn't see, knocked against telephone poles, hydrants, the gas lamps.

"Please . . ." he cried, "please. . . ." Only it was too late, he was pulled, knees skinning, up the long flight of stone steps.

"Wipe it off!" The cop shoved a white handkerchief into the phlegm and tears plastered over his face. "Say your prayers," the policeman ordered, took hold again of his elbow. They walked through the heavy doors into the vestibule, into the gray vault, down a side aisle. He was pushed into the confession box.

As he bitterly wept, blew into the handkerchief, he heard, "What's the matter?" a soft, friendly voice.

"Tell me all about it . . . ohhh . . . ohhh . . ." sweet, a whisper punctuating his confused talk, tears.

". . . Ohhh . . . ohhh," like the fuzzy tick tock of an old clock, ". . . ohh . . . ohhh . . . ohhh, that's not so bad . . . ohhh, it's all right now . . .

"Ohhh. . . ."

A hand touched his knee.

Gogarty sleepily looked up.

"Relax," Ark said, stroking him.

Gogarty saw rainbows of green, blue, red, rippling over the rumpled sheets.

A breeze blew from the air-shaft window through the bathroom door into the bedroom. The moans and splashing had stopped and he heard only their heavy breathing, his own, a crackling rainbow.

"Aw, cut it out," he mumbled, "cut it out."

Civic Colosseum rises out of the murky waters of a garbage channel. Tier on tier of cement, its Roman arches climb from an indentation of Newark Bay, that long, foul backwater of the Atlantic which seeps behind the rusty city fronts—Bayonne, Jersey City, Hoboken—facing Manhattan. In a wilderness of scrap yards, dust heaps and abandoned factories, the Colosseum is the sole height. Night and day a wind of gas and ash blows over these acres and truckers roll up their windows as they ride quickly through the district.

From the stadium, across the chemical waters of the bay, one can see the bowed cranes of empty shipyards whose only work is tearing apart the ancient Liberty ships, red and rusting at their docks, ready to fall apart without the creaking demolition apparatus. Old wooden tugs slowly soak up water here and, sodden, sink beneath the waves.

Bleak rubbish, graveyard of World War One troop trains, discarded Hudson ferries, gutted trucks, the docks along the bay crumbling back into its edge of slime; over all this, the Colosseum. Huge, squat, a concrete memento to three men of the adjoining cities who died in the Spanish-American War.

The North Jersey shore shook off the Depression building this white elephant. A few minor-league games played there. One or two drum-majorette contests a year. A seedy circus. Stock-car races that tore up the turf followed by a bankrupt rodeo giving last shows.

For years now it has sat boarded with shutters and scrap wood to shut out the gangs of teenage hoods, walls scrawled with obscenities, concrete cracking, old and ugly with the smog of Newark Bay, a crypt.

It is the site of the great national convention of the Continentals. For the past few weeks workmen have been preparing the building. A plastic bubble has converted it to an all-weather auditorium. Swarms of Continentals arriving have camped out in the abandoned factories, shipyards, troop trains and ferries. Hotel facilities are filled. The road to the Colosseum is choked with traffic, thousands and thousands of cars and the bus from the subway which brings Dora and O'Dougherty toward the stadium makes its way inch by inch among stalled vehicles.

"You're nuts!" Dora screamed in the dim bus interior jammed with uniforms.

"I've got the whole wo-orld in my hands!" cried O'Dougherty.

"You didn't call! Let's get off. Turn him in!"

"Why don't you?"

"You're the man!"

O'Dougherty shook his head. She felt lumps rise in her throat. Her limbs ached. Something had bitten her. The vampire flowed in her veins. How had he got those fingerprints? Had he? Who sent him? Was he part of it? He was . . . Freakish, the whole thing, the people on the bus blurred, O'Dougherty's face.

"No."

"You just came for the show." She struck out to claw him.

He caught her hand, laughing. "The greatest show on earth."

three

Circus! Circus! Circus! Everyone out of the way. Make room. A world is dashing in. Here come tigers, lions, elephants, huge gray beasts, striped cats, roaring kings and queens, all stampeding through acres of sticky pink sugar candy, clouds of it billowing in the dust of the arena.

For children? Only if children are closer to joy, terror, excitement. Sitting with them on our knees, wiping the confectionery from our lips, do we feel in their pounding heartbeat, the danger of the animals, the daring of the high-wire ballet, the hope of the human cannon?

Sideshows, shills, freaks, what are they doing here? Is this a child's entertainment? What is going on? Why bring the little ones to a spectacle where they are continually shrieking with fear or gaping, amazed, encouraged, at the forbidding sights, the grotesques.

Beasts—what are they doing here? Are they not in display at every decent city zoo? Why does the trainer go among them in his costume, pith hat and pantaloons, snapping the barbed edge of the whip, forcing into human posture through outlandish tricks? What unnatural parody of beasthood do these snarling tigers and lions perform, counting, juggling, mountebanking?

The little ones hold their breath knowing that the man is tiny, despite his whip, his gun, he is inside the bars, a moment now, the ferocious cats will tire of the silly game, go back to savagery, overwhelm the upright figure in their sleek, rippling, deadly midst, tear it to shreds.

Behold the elephant, titanic, balancing his weight in scant dresses, a ballerina, three feet in the air, trumpeting hysteria, jungle laughter, will he not at last let his big foot down and crush to silken, fleshly tatters the crinoline miss who prods him with a stick?

The babies, row on row, cry, shaking delirious cones of cotton sugar, go mad, mad with hope. And the clowns whistle and toot among them to divert their joy and terror.

No?

Why bring them then through alleys filled with freaks, monsters, misshapen horrors? The fat lady waves to them, gross, bulbous, her flesh rank with glandular fury, spreading on her stool, a hippopotamus.

In defiance of his suicide, the sword swallower stabs at the innards, gulps down fire, mechanically performs the rites of holy men. No less striking is his neighbor, the woman with a beard, initiation to the hermaphrodite. Even the strong man, an archaic creature, so bound in muscles, he grunts and groans more animal than man. Twelve-fingered, two-headed, stunted, gigantic, four-footed, sprouting tails, Humanity displays itself as it splits and bursts into strange, inhuman forms.

And if you herd the children forward quickly through these ancient sights? Once inside the tent . . .

Above their heads flash specks of white, tossing, twisting, somersaulting, flying from pole to pole in the glare of the long, graceful searchlights. The slip of a hand, a toe, far

And there is no net? Why? Why? The thing has repeated itself so many times it is a credible certainty.

The whole act is ruined, stale, dull, flat, all the grace, excitement, artistry gone out of it, all the joy of the spectators, unless it takes place over the bare, hard dirt or concrete floor hundreds of feet below.

The little ones stare up, waiting.

No?

The human cannoneer!

Yes, there is a net to catch him. But that was never what I thought, sitting at six or seven, mouth sticky with caramel and crackerjack. The feat was impossible. I did not want it to succeed.

He would explode in the thick, black cannon and be shot out in a blast of bones, hair, blood and clothes all over our faces.

What else through the tedious repetition of the performances, music, announcements, jokes, keeps the babies up so far past their bedtime? Half-asleep, they stay awake, dreaming, praying for the shadowed, slithering antagonist to win the death-defying act, just once, a miss, a failure. . . .

O children, O circuses, among you survive the rhythms, mystery, festivals we have refused to celebrate. We leave behind in you more than our innocence, our wisdom, our memories of an older knowledge and its rites.

"Man does not live by bread alone." Ay! "*Panem et circenses!* Bread and circuses!" cried the Roman mob. "Impossible to control the populace without them." Not enough to be at the center of an empire, its wealth, no, there must be some terrible celebration and parody, a mockery of the *Pax*. And it must grow more and more elaborate as the bureaucracy of the empire spreads, as the comforts of the *Pax* increase, as the frontiers of war retreat. At first the Circus Maximus will do. Under the republic, a simple triumph, the procession of priests, virgins, the bobbing Legion standards, captured prisoners, unusual trophies.

One hundred and seventy-five holidays a year.

Under the emperor, life jades. The Colosseum rises for the agonies, its walls purple with victims dashed, torn, beasts, men, machines, eating, feasting on each other under the waning sun. The citizens in the open stands, their wives high above, under striped silk awnings, leaning forward to taste the gory bread. Sea battles are floated forth, real arrows, real fire, real death rages under the hungry eye of the mob. The dignitaries walk the fragile barrier, the podium, privileged to be closest, to be entertained by the possibility of being overwhelmed; the tigers, bears, spears leap into the spectators to draw them into the spectacle.

Where is the stage? Where is the audience? Let us crowd into the street of those Greek towns, frenzied, tearing at our clothes, flailing leather penises, exposing ourselves, jumping on each other, women, men, animals.

We have pushed down these acts in the damp beds of adolescence, thrust back, trussed, drugged. Even our curiosity is stilled.

Yes, the Church rose, the voice of reason, law, justice, the noblest thought of Jerusalem, Athens, Rome. Moses, Paul, Mohammed, Luther, turning their parishioners in upon themselves, their thoughts, turning all the ceremonies to rites of guilt. Guilt, guilt, all our ingenious, rational structures built on it. Even when the syphilitic prophet proclaimed that God was dead, he drove us forward along the same path, overcome, overdo, go beyond oneself. Man is above man.

And if Man is below man?

"Take your hand out of your pocket!" as the barker, eye acock, snaps at the burlesque (which is another chapter, but enough).

Circuses rise and fall.

In this century, 2,000 years after Christ, it seemed as if the edifice of Protestant logic was breaking up. Yes, Protestant. The cardinal whose death I noted earlier, was as much a descendant of Calvin as Leo. Grasping his flock tight by the scruff of guilt, he had brought them regularly to the abstraction of bread and wine. Only in the last years of his reign things were coming undone. Priests had begun to experiment on their own. The building of authority in the Church itself was cracking. In America at large there was a general sense of silliness about the clergy. Naturally the latter busied themselves immediately with good works to justify their existence and ride out the era, the storm. Only the spirit blew more powerfully. People were religious. Only they were experimenting. In the meadows of the great municipalities, parks, large numbers met to exchange vows of love and chant together. They sang in a polygot of traditions which they only half-understood, but underneath perhaps the impulse was genuine. And as the sun went down and they paired off to roll together in the park bushes, it seemed to many as if they had touched something real. Banners, costumes, unconventional behavior; these familiar traits characterized the gatherings. The press was strangely attracted to them.

So, many of us, respectable, sober, middle-class, found ourselves sitting that year beside our children at the Big Show. Where previously we might have sent them with a baby sitter, governess, now we attended in person, staring, not as usual, bored, distracted, fussing with the kiddies' clothes or irritably correcting their manners; no, almost oblivious of the tots, throughout the huge auditoriums and gardens of America, we sat rapt, absorbed in the panoply below. Delighting in the gray bulk of the elephants, shining with fiery bits of colored glass in their elaborate harness, hearing the screams of the Romans cast under their monstrous hooves, the tread of the herd that trampled the hapless deserters of Paulus' army. Seeing the bears, clumsy, humorous, rising as they did of old, prodded in the rectum with hot irons, starving, amid piercing cries to flail the faces, bellies of huddling Christians. The lesser animals, that menagerie, pigs, dogs, ponies, jumping, tumbling, clowning forth, dressed, trained like men, boys, girls. One cannot forbear to mention Herodotus: *The Histories,* Book Two, describing the Pan-struck Mendesians, who held all goats in veneration. "In this province not long ago a goat tupped a woman, in full view of everybody—surprising."

And though the tots blink and begin to nod, we stare up into the blazing lights of the ceiling, watching the bodies springing hand to hand, looping, circling, in that dark space, a night pinpointed with lamps, lit up in the full moons of the searchlights; seeing the sequins of the trapeze artists glint in the impossible flight, defying gravity, from fragile swing to swing, clasping with precise touch a second, at the hands, ankles, of a mate; we lifted our children's prayer, entreating that one of those bright stars shall fail, miss, fall.

O Lucifer!

Mother-of-pearl, imitation, he gripped the handle. A fuckin' circus! The whole goddamn act was comin' apaht in his hands. He had grabbed the shooting iron from a midget in the corridor, a little guy in a 20-gallon cowboy hat, elevator boots and leather chaps that trailed behind him. Paul Gogarty reached into the pipsqueak's holster and pulled the oversize pistol out. The three and a half feet screamed and cursed. "It's loaded, you ffff . . . frigging ffff . . . freak!"

The midget tried to bite him, but Paul rapped the shortie in the teeth with the steel barrel and kicked him back, blood-mouthed, against the wall. Furious, he strode on, shoving the long iron down deep in his pants pocket.

His brother, the senator, had just had him on the phone upstairs. Senile prick! Who the hell was he, playin' the gray eminence, the statesman? "Better get out of this. It stinks. They got the goods on him."

The fuckin' Jesuit. He had the goods on him, too. He had been pissin' the Boston bookie receipts into his campaigns for fohty years now.

The most powerful bastard in Congress, standin' right behind the President, and he was a basket case. He could hahdly say a sentence straight, tellin' him, "It stinks."

He felt the tears, hot, in the corners of his eyes. The senile old bastahd was right. That shit-eatin' asshole, the general, had rung up a minute later, practically cut right into the line to tell him to take his name off the list, out of the organization. It was going to be in the papers.

Paul going weak between the legs. Losing control. He was trying to hold on to his bladder, but as the general drove it home, the trickle started down his leg, more and more, until he was pissing as hard as he could into the black wool of his own pants.

"Can't we stop it?" he asked.

The pompous fuckin' idiot gave him ten seconds of silence and began to roast him. ". . . Stop it? If I had known . . . Don't you ever . . . I'm going to make sure . . . you and your . . ." As if he didn't have any stink of his own. The asshole had made 15 landings in the last war on the same island for the sake of the photographers.

"Who the hell are you?" he finally shouted back into the receiver. "You shit out the same end as me."

Silence.

"What am I supposed to do? Huh? Huh?"

Paul laughed, then shivered. The answer came back in a cold, clipped voice.

The black club dropped back into its box.

He was sick. He wanted to puke. The phone started ringing again. A secretary answered it. The calls were coming in fast. The Mafia wanted to know what was up, the officers at some of the veterans' organizations heard a rumor, etc., etc. "Tell 'em to cut it out," he barked across the room to the secretary. "They got ants in their pants. They wanna staht somethin'? Some Commie is tryin' to staht a stampede. Last-minute crap, it always happens. Tell 'em to go back to sleep."

He tried out a hearty laugh on the girl, coughed it up out of his throat. "Jokahs . . ." he mumbled, bending down, pretending to tie a shoelace: slipped a jackknife out and cut the phone line. He rose from his seat, grinning, then walked backwards to the door, chuckling, dreading she would see the drip, drip, down his pants leg.

He had to hold it off. If the word got out to that friggin' bunch of zombies here in the stadium, they would tear the fuckin' walls apart. They were hopped up as is. Two or three guys had been tossed out the windows of their hotels at the parties last night. Just for a joke, they had tried to lynch one of the Hawaiian delegation this morning and an honor guard had to push through the drunken crowd with fixed bayonets to cut him down. Who knows how the mother-fuckers would take it? They had burned down a baseball park in Duluth just because the speakers were an hour late.

There must be some way to get the bastahds outta here. They were gettin' restless. A report had come up to the office on top of the stadium that some of the boys were rippin' out the plumbing in the men's room. Another story about a gang bang in the ladies' comfort station.

O Jesus, if this broke . . .

Screamin', tearin' their uniforms, running half-naked through the corridors, a gang of fruits, locos, weirdies. Firebugs lightin' up the cups and newspapers under their seats, dousin' whomever they could with lighter fluid. A niggah from Chicago had been burned to death about an hour ago in a utility closet. There was a kike limpin' around with a charred ankle a few minutes latah, screamin' about some kids from New York City.

The whole place would be up in flames. Shit, they'd melt the girders off the ceilin'. That Plexiglas shield on top would go like cellophane. It was gonna be a goddamn hellhole. That crowd was roarin' to go.

If they got their hands on him—they'd yank his balls off. He had to get down to that room. He had to head things off. He started to run.

Holy Christ! The sweat started out on his forehead, the heat, itching, had started again between his legs. He could smell the stink. Fuckin' wool pants. It would be hours befoh they dried. He didn't have a change of underwear. The drawers he soaked this afternoon were his last. He should have snatched a pair of panties off that midget. He could have stretched them or something. The little guy's boots came up to his gonads. He probably wore oversized drawers.

Holy! Holy! They were scratchin' and burnin'. Boils were breaking out again. He had to get them off. Ripping off the buttons of his fly, he reached into his pants and tore at the damp linen. Pulling out a handful, he threw it behind him in the corridor. The relief lasted seconds. It was worse. His testicles brushed against the raw wool. At each stride he was flayed by the steely fibers. He slowed down, taking a step at a time. Mother! Get me outta this! He had a bed of thorns in there. Every time he lifted his foot, it was tortchah. Peeling off the last of the cotton, he thrust his free hand down and tried to shield his bags, cupping them as he walked.

Everything was in shreds. The whole fuckin' ohganization. He had been runnin' around for the last three years settin' it up, collaring this one and that, every crackpot bunch in the country was "affiliated," every special interest and lobby had been given promises. He had so many deals goin' he couldn't remember half o' them. Everybody was about to come out foh Star. They had the bandwagon piled so high with pork barrel it would have rolled all over the country. Nothing would have stood up against it. Down in that stadium he had piled an army up, right and left. Conservatives, radicals, anyone who wanted a slice of the pie. New Left, Old Right, he had them kissin' each other's asses.

It was goddamn beautiful. It was so perfect he had practically cried every time he thought about it. And now the bandwagon was high and dry up shit's creek. Every bugger he had called would be ready to murder him.

He groaned. His ass was on fire. In the last year he had signed up dozens of blue-ribbon blue-ribbons, the respectable idiots. Backslapping, he enrolled FBI men, CIA types, unions, Chambers of Commerce, Anti-Defamation Leagues. Half the fuckin' country was gonna be caught with its pants down.

Paul thrashed through Continentals, twisting and turning in his trousers as he pushed down the concrete ramps toward the bottom of the stadium. The black uniforms that wandered as groups of two or three dozen, higher up, flowed at this lower level back and forth in one crush. They were dammed between the counters of the hot-dog stands and the doors of the comfort stations. He had to batter a way through the beery crowd with his shoulders. One hand was in his crotch, the other deep in his pocket. The pearl swirls of the steer horns carved in the soft palm flesh. He held the stock tight.

Next week he would have been pulling the gut strings.

He ground his flesh into the steer horns, tore his bags away from the sticky side of the pants. His whole fuckin' career.

He had fought his way up from the scuttles, dragging that creep his brother along, from a two-room flat with a washtub full of coal, a backyard of garbage, torn sheets on the clotheslines. His father face down on the kitchen table, floundering, whiskey pouring out of his gills. Their little four-foot mother trying to bang some life into him with a frying pan. Two rooms, always filled with out-of-luck cousins, fighting your way in the morning across a floor sprawled with whores, winos, jokers on the run from the cops. He had yanked that skinny half-wit, his brother, still drooling, out of there into the street, looking for work, shoeshine, newspaper boy, clerk, runnin' errands for pols.

The almighty buck, fuckin' green, God bless it.

None of that *thou shalt not* crap, not when you could walk up the Hill and see a bunch of bluenoses sittin' on a pile. It smelled good up there. And no one was gonna keep him down in the trough smellin' shit.

He had cracked noodles, broken bones, pushed his opponents out of windows, off piers. A free country! If you had power, brains. He beat that right into the thin skull of his brother. Robbing the grocery store they clerked in, slipping through the back door at night with a double he made of the key; then shaking down the shoeshine, the newspaper boys, burning the headquarters of the candidate he was handing out leaflets for. You wrote the rules.

If you licked up what they pissed in your face, that was your problem. Everyone in the trough smelled, crawlin' off to church Sunday to get a whiff of perfume on their ass.

Money, power would take the smell off. He watched the cardinal and his boys climbing up the Hill. Get up there! Get a hunk! He pushed the ninny into elections, hired a gang to tear down the other guy's signs, beat up his supporters. He dropped five-dollar bills into the laps of all the neighborhood big mouths. He had a picture taken of the parish priest accepting a huge (rubber) check, a Gogarty button pinned in his cassock. And when the other guy cried foul, he threw dirt on him. "A turncoat. He sold his vote. He screws his sister-in-law. He's an atheist. A queer. You name it!"

He smothered the guy under a pile. And his brother had that pious look, worth a million, Oh, I just come from assistin' at the sacred act of transubstantiation, I'm so holy, you mustn't touch me, please.

Christ! The suckers ate it up. He sang how they were gonna chase the fuckin' Yankees out of the state, give a hundred dollars from the treasury to every Irishman, able-bodied or not, rain shamrock over the ward; while slippin' up the Hill for a big contribution—a few votes sold in advance. Yankees, filthier you were, the more they loved you. They had the goods on you.

They were on top of you. Pullin' the strings, their clubs, colleges, banks. Even the governor had to get on the phone with 'em. Noddin' his head like a nigger.

You hadda turn that power in. Well, he was through with that. This ohganization was goin' right up without 'em. He had the strings. And when he got on top . . .

Washington, D.C., Internal Revenue, the Army, tanks, bombs, taxes, let it fly. A ton of shit.

All those assholes who had their faces in the crap, get their heads out of it, get them moving, on the march.

Blow the fuckin' horn. Down the Ohio, the Wabash, the Mississippi, up the Missouri, the Red, the Arkansas, across the Continental Divide, from the topmost peak of the Berkshires, to the tip of Cape Cod: they were marching, assholes, millions of 'em, every shape and size.

He was pullin' up a tent pole and the canvas would spread from coast to coast, that old-time religion.

Paul seized the stock of his gun.

Momma! Momma! He was crying, ready to squeeze it off in his pocket. Shoot off his balls.

They had shafted him. They drove the pole right up his rear. When the news hit the papers, he was through. There wasn't a Knights of Vespucius post in America that would let him walk past the entrance. They'd laugh him out of every bar he'd ever drunk in. The white horse, he used to get up on to lead the Saint Patrick's Day parade, the silver-hilted sword from the Knights, his chest dangling with ribbons, medals, orders, the fancy hat, breeches, after-dinner speeches, glory, over. Over, over, over, over. . . .

"Bastahds, dihty bastahds!"

He began pushing forward, his crotch entangled with barbed wire, screaming out loud in the corridor. It was a fuckin' plot. They had done it purposely, leaked that news. They were out to get him. That Star was a stooge. Those pricks had ganged up on him to ruin his fuckin' connections. They drove Dole off his rocker. The reverend had been bought out, a small-town operator, he'd sell his own sister down the river for a buck. Ark!

He should have known better than to get mixed up with that half-queer. You could never figure his angle, that smile of his. He was behind it somehow. Screwing him right in the ass.

"Holy shit!"

Paul yanked at his trousers. The crowd was shoving him. He

threw himself forward. He had to get down to that room, to Star. The fuckahs were gonna put his picture on the front page of every daily, the snapshot of him running around bare-assed last night. He jerked open his fly. They were gonna make a fuckin' queer joke out of him.

He was in flames below. "O sacred mother! Stop!" Snatching the damp cloth in his crotch, he tore the pants down, ripping them off one leg, then the other. He flung the two pieces aside. "I'll kill him!"

He screamed, digging, clawing with his free hand through the packed corridor, waving the pistol in the air. That evil prick knew he was about to dump him. That's why he started that thing last night, gave the speech this morning. He was crazy. The bastahd was out to destroy him, everything.

"I'll kill him!" he screamed again, slashing with the butt of his gun.

"Jesus!" someone shouted. "The guy has no pants. Hey! They stole his shorts, too."

On both sides of Paul the mob started to hoot and howl. A hand snatched at his bags. Another yanked his penis. Fingers were pulling at his hairs. "Get away from me! Get the fuck away!"

He shot down into the crowd.

Blood spattered the faces around him. On all sides the black bodies fought, arms flailing, to get out of the way. Blind with pain, he drove through them, feeling his way along the hall. He pushed himself through a fire exit, stumbled down a narrow, winding iron staircase, and bolted along a deserted ramp toward the room on the stadium floor, running, bumping the walls, his private parts swinging free, huge, swollen, dripping with blood.

Ark had told him. It was all over. They knew. Except that he had known for months. It had to be. There was no anger in him. No. It was a relief. Although the fear of what was to come was thick in his throat, a lump he could taste, breathe against, knowing for sure set him free to dream a few seconds, to recall what had blurred in the march of the last few months.

It seemed as if he had been always dreaming this, living it.

Now, sitting here in the huge band room, empty, hearing the continuing roar of the crowd beyond the heavy doors that swung open onto the floor of the arena, the sound louder, angrier moment by moment as they waited for his entrance, delayed; the bands had gone out, the drill teams, the comedy acts; they were waiting for the speakers; Dole had run off; Gogarty was still upstairs; Billy Jim and Ark were waiting for him here; sitting here, in the room here he discovers himself, motionless, one set of fingers folded, locked into the other pair, one eye on his right, one on his left, two nostrils, two feet, two testic . . . feet, arms, legs, minds.

Two.

There were two of him.

He was here and not here.

Who was here?

Thine is the Kingdom. On earth as it is in Heaven. As it is

written, behold, I send my Messenger. Signs and Wonders. The Son of Man.

Of Man.

His fingers held one another. His body, manhood, mortified. That one he was still.

His fingers, he remembered, sitting by the table, hands locked together, tight-fisted, pious.

The woman, his mother, saying again and again, psalm after psalm, shouting them out, hours and hours, up straight, repeating, repeating, staring ahead until he could make out one by one the lilies of the fading wallpaper, some running with the ripple of rust in the wall, others dried scraps, flaking off, whole parts of the field buckled, caving in. Garden of the east, the house tilting down over a crumbling foundation.

The stone which the builders rejected, become, the chief cornerstone.

Look through the broken windowpanes, past the outhouse on its side, the gray collapsed barn, fields going to seed, the sky: praying, the sky, the sky, sky, sky, sky.

The dove came to him at eventide, and lo, in her mouth.

Across the table, his sister began to cry.

The first forefinger crossed the second forefinger.

The sister.

The index fingers crossed. The thumbs made an x. Touch me not!

For all was soon to be made holy, pure, he would ascend.

They were stomping, a steady drumming on the concrete tiers of the stadium. Mockers, tormentors. He had heard the beer cans crashing down on the bands, the foul cries, the awful purgatory through which he must go.

Beyond that. He must think of the promises. The glory, light that would stream forth as he rose from dark forests of agony on high.

He looked at Ark, Billy Jim. They were frightened, smiling, but the sound beyond the doors, echoing in the cavernous, still room, unsettled them.

His sister.

No. He had passed that. He must not think of it. All shadows, vague, a dream he had to suffer.

It had been confirmed, made plain, these last years. He had seen it in their eyes as he traveled from post to post. Cloudy, sheepish, bewildered, they leaned forward, trying to understand, to see.

And he, speaking, letting the words go out, blurted, stumbling, one by one, until suddenly he hit one, the key, and they moaned, and words, others, followed, and they moaned together, saw it, understood, and he went faster, then faster, carrying them, moving them, higher, higher, until they, he, were screaming, seeing, seeing.

He broke off. Those words, the miracle, only half-aware of them now, what they were. You gave yourself, surrendered, a force.

Would melt them, you, all, until there was just one presence, stirring, consuming, all in the room.

That was part of it.

The other he had seen afterwards, the spit at the corners of their mouths as he broke off; the shaking in their seats, cow, dog, horse sounds. In the small posts they tore down curtains, smashed windows, pissed on the floor, shit on each other, burning, destroying.

Destruction following destruction. The whole land spoiled.

Now behind the doors they were rising to grasp at the lapels before them in the crammed bleachers, thrusting thumbs, fingernails into eyeballs, knuckles into jaws, forcing their hands into the mouth, jerking it back and forth, digging, breaking, pulling asunder. Swarming with ice picks, scissors, razors, at cheeks, ears, noses. Switchblades, swords, black bodies hacking, cleaving, blood, blood. Let them draw forth streams, rivers. A torrent, spurting, foaming, a lake over eyes, mouths, black, black, O

White, White

"Sign it."

The nurse, fat, dumpy, a stained linen cap pinned to her hair, red wires, bent over him. The silvery, older doctor, Borden, leaning down, too. They had strapped him in the bed. "Here's your chance."

He heard the snickers, two doctors more.

"Walk out of here tomorrow."

The nurse stuck a pen in his hand.

Gleaming, white-toothed, the Puerto Rican internes, he had heard of them, the operations.

He tried to pull his hand away, but she forced it down on the paper.

". . . or else."

"What?"

They laughed. He saw the smile on Dr. Borden's face. The nurse pushed, the pen made the first stroke of his name.

"Here, take this!" The doctor forced a pill in his mouth, one of those . . . made you drowsy . . . pushed you . . . down . . . into sleep.

Only he woke, in a sweat, just as they were taking him on a stretcher into the operating room. He was bound hand and foot on the narrow cot, but he began to struggle, yanking a wrist free, then a foot, trying to topple himself out. They fell on him, the nurse, the doctor, the internes, attendants, hitting him in the face with their fists. And he knew what they were going to do.

"No!" he cried. "No!"

The screams died away in the empty band room.

Ark and Billy Jim were looking at him hard, grinning. "Nervous?"

He shook his head.

"Want a tranquilizer?"

He shook it again, jerking angrily, staring up at the ceiling. It was high, half the height of the stadium. Almost 2,000 musicians had been standing, jammed in there an hour ago. Now it was empty except for three figures, vast, a mausoleum. The gray paint peeled from the walls. Old bunting streaked with dirt, drooped in patches against the walls, hanging down hundreds of feet, ragged. He was seated on a milk box, overturned.

How had he come? Who had brought him?

Ark, Billy Jim, they had prepared a bitter draught for him, gall and wormwood.

Yet he might turn it aside. Upstairs in his suitcase there was the costume, a blouse, slacks, short wig, lipstick. He could flee as he had before, unnoticed through the crowds, abandoning the procession, taking another, easier way. A few hours ago it had been a game, a disguise. Yet he could become what he wanted. He could leave at any point, the cross, get out from under, even now. Ark had told him that.

They were waiting.

For what?

The sacred hour, now approaching, he must forget the game, the dreams, drive away the thoughts of that other life, thinking only of the exacting glory of the task before him, its height, depth, ascension.

He that hath clean hands and a pure heart.

Ark had started it last night. Daring him to put it on, dance, show what he could do. They had drunk too much. His dignity . . . gross . . .

Who was he?

O Father, he prayed. Let me go up on your holy mountain. Let me ascend into your place. Open your gates, O you everlasting doors, let me come in. For I shall sit on the right hand. I shall come up covered with glory. The whole earth is full of it. Father, take me up. Now! Now! With chariot, cries, angels, stirring of wings, cymbals, hymns, Father, now, now!

He stretched his hands up, rising on the milk box.

There was no answer.

He shivered.

Before—he had heard, had promises. Lifting himself in prayer, the voice ringing in his ear, he felt the presence, the spirit, an answer in the strength that surged through his body. He wanted to turn, blazing with it, to Ark, Billy Jim, give them their answer, to go forth possessed, shaking with zeal, holy.

Now, his hands crooked, limp in the air, he knew they were staring. He looked funny, stupid. Only he had to—without it—

Father, he began.

Father.

Father.

The words, his thoughts would not go that way. Instead a face, they groped to reconstruct. Vague, familiar, he could not recall it.

The cracked gray tabletop, broken legs; it tipped to one side, then the other, as you leaned.

Fingers, his own were small, dirty, the nails chewed, spread out on the weather-beaten wood beside a chipped blue bowl.

Opposite him, tiny toy thumbs, a palm still soft with baby fat, tracing out circles on the wet wooden boards.

His mother's, long-jointed, crabbed, red, stiff, at the table's edge, then jumping to her bowl, spoon, the baby's hand.

A pair of sunburned hands rested on the pitted gray wood, the nails split, ridged, the fingers huge, each as large as three or four of his, thick black hairs tangled above, below the joints, across the back. They moved slowly off the table, fell into a lap. The face was kind, yet not there, away from the three of them, determined, set in the deep lines around the mouth.

The taste of the milk, crisp flakes of cereal, the bowl, those strong hands, the sense of them on the table, the face, the smile at him, his sister; a second, then it faded as he grasped trying to reach out, hold the huge fingers, they faded, Father, Father.

He lost it. And thought he found it again. Although it was lined, deeper, older, not smiling but wincing, disgusted.

He crouched naked on the floor, bowels bloody, blinded by floodlights, the costume strewn across the room in rags, the old cop, the sergeant who had driven his tormentors off, bending down, listening as he talked, couldn't stop, the words pushing through tears, telling how, about his sister, touching her, the asylum, the vision, Ark, the masquerade. And choking, as he tried to say why, explain, he recognized the hands. Looked up into the face.

O God, God. He was not who he was. Father. Out there they would tear him to bits. Why had he come here? They knew. Why? Ark! Ark! He clawed the air. Billy Jim laughed, crowing, a cock.

He would go up. The gates. As it was foretold. Clean, clean. He rubbed his hands. On earth as it is in Heaven. I'm coming! I'm coming! Clubs, clubs, battered at him. Stop. O God, stop. Filth, gore, pushing his face into his own shit. O Father, Father. At thy right hand. Forgive them. The everlasting gates. Up! Up! I will. Will! Ark!

Ark!

He was standing now, pointing across the cavern at him, seeing the actor through misted eyes, waking from a dream. "I will!" he had shouted. The figure was drifting in the fog of his head.

Why?

O, he brought his hands to his face, covering his eyes, seeing, in the darkness, he was the victim. It was through his blood that they would be absolved, purged. It was an act, a sacrifice, the evil in the land fathered through him, sown, reaped, gathered now, the madness like a festering, an infection, lanced in his body. It had been set up.

No! He would not. It was not how it was supposed to be. What he had been told, the promises. He would not go.

Only if he fled . . . to what? He had to have . . . to be. It was true.

O Father, Father. Help me. Help me.

At this extremest hour. Help, for I come. . . . "Help me!" His voice was hoarse. "Help me! Help!"

He was there, still standing, in the band room.

It was all over. Over, over, over, over.

"I'm going, okay?"

"I'm going!"

Ark made no move as he walked, began to run toward the tiny back door.

It flew open.

"You fuckin' son of a bitch!"

"Paul!" they cried behind him. Boils, eyes, nose, a flaming shape tore at itself in the doorway, fire licking at black hairs, rod shaking in its hand.

Red, red, he fell back before the curses. The rod exploded.

Once. Billy Jim, clown white, swayed, one hand on his head, the other at his belt.

Twice. Ark, running backwards to the great doors, wheeled, furious, clutching his breast. "Aim!" he shrieked. "Aim!"

Another explosion rang out.

It fell upon him. The rod smashed in his teeth. He grasped the end of it, trying to push away the oily, steaming rot, the angel of sweat, shit, his hand pressed into the hot, clammy blood, toppling onto the floor, wrestling.

Just before the fourth explosion, before the darkness, he heard, above the murderous curses, trumpets, golden, glorious, the sound of the gates rolling, the thunderous roar, and the light, O Father, the light, light, flooding, light bursting upon him.

They had been wandering for hours, trying to get in. At gate after gate O'Dougherty showed his press card. The attendants shook their heads. No reporters.

Thousands and thousands of Continentals were trooping through. O'Dougherty and Dora in civilian clothes stood out, violent bright spots in the black throng. Twice or three times, he couldn't remember, they had walked around the endless circumference of the stadium, hoping to slip through unnoticed or persuade a guard to let them in. O'Dougherty had folded almost 40 dollars in single five-dollar bills into the palms of gate attendants. Stone-faced, they pocketed it, but barred the way. His feet were sore, the arches cramped, a blister rubbed at his ankle. He was sweating like a long-distance runner as they trudged on to the next gate.

Dora, more hysterical at each stop, was staring ahead now, saying nothing. She moved slowly, languid, her hands rose, heavily, in a stupor, to brush the hair back from her brow. Her breasts pushed against him, growing larger.

He stopped and touched her forehead. It was hot. "You all right?"

She nodded, her cheeks flushed. Her breath was steaming.

O'Dougherty cursed. Why hadn't he brought uniforms for them? He should have known.

Go and file the story, he told himself. Why are you here? It was crazy.

Pulling Dora's glowing arm, he struck to the side with an elbow, wedging through the black drove, thrashing, muttering excuse me's, toward the gate ahead. He held his credentials out in front of him. This was the last time.

From within the stadium came the din of noisemakers, laughter, hooting, louder than the buzzing as the crowd pressed outside the iron palings. Judging from the hilarity that rang from the open spaces of the arches, wild pranks were going on. The merriment even spread through the gates. People around them in fits, hiccuping with laughter. O'Dougherty could not help smiling as he got up to the paling.

The attendant broke into an ear-splitting guffaw, was just about to stop and turn the two of them back. Two fingers thrust out from behind the gateman's back. They grasped O'Dougherty's hand. Shook it vigorously.

"Hi, kids!" O'Dougherty could not see the speaker. "Yew fergit yer yewniforms?"

The fingers pulled him through the gate, Dora behind him. "My friends. Just let 'em on in."

A face flashed out. O'Dougherty recognized it. Something pushed into his hand. "Put 'em on, kids. Yew won't have no trouble."

He looked down, two black caps, a Continental medal pinned to each, the ribbon blue in the man's, red in the woman's.

He looked up but the face was gone. Dora recognized someone, too. He saw a moustache, a large nose, sinking into the heads before them, a second later someone tossed the nose and moustache up into the air. Dora shivered, her limbs trembling, the grippe. "You're sick," said O'Dougherty. "Let's get out of here."

Only it was too late. The crowd began to move faster into the Colosseum. They could not fight the current and were dragged across the yard through the doors into the vaulted lobby of the bottom floor. O'Dougherty clung to Dora, afraid she would be torn out of his grasp. Her hand burned in his.

"Hold on!" he called. "Hold!"

A rip tide had started to move through the packed black caps. O'Dougherty, standing on tiptoe, could just see the shallow trough dipping before its crest as it forced the bodies to bend before it, carrying them in its wake: a ripple, 30 or 40 feet wide, flowing through the lobby, not disturbing the main body but only those in its path. Helpless, O'Dougherty saw it coming their way, felt the push pressing him down, then the pull drawing him forward.

He was at the edge of the rip and Dora was being drawn in the other direction. Twisting his free hand out of the press, he grasped her arm with both his and tried to tug her toward him. The rip was dragging him on, away from her. He heard her cry as, desperate, he dug his fingers into her slipping arm. Then suddenly Dora, too, was caught, knocked, jammed up against him.

In each other's arms, they were twisted into the bodies moving up a ramp. Dora's breasts burst out, breaking the buttons of her dress, bulging from her brassiere, the nipples pressed into his chest, wood plugs. Her knee slid between his legs. Her lips, moist, fevered, through the bubbles of spit, swam on his. His hand went to the back of her dress. He found not the tight cloth of her dress but panties, and the flesh of her buttocks.

A hand was at his prick, touching it, and it leaped, struck in his pants, at his zipper. He felt the fly going down, the trousers falling.

Jesus, he was out, bounding. A finger in: her crack was running, oily, torrential. Her hands went around his neck. She was hoisting herself up on him, her thighs apart, his—oh, he couldn't believe—going in. And he reared, arched. . . .

"Aaaaaaahhh . . ." the crowd swirled on the ramp, wrenching Dora off, away, he caught at her hand, his pants.

"Sssss . . . sson of a bbbb . . . bitch!" a shrill voice shrieked above the whirlpool. O'Dougherty was squeezed into the spinning circle. About a dozen men were bending down in the center. A midget, one legged, hopped in their midst.

"He bbb . . . bit me!" the creature squealed. The foot he held in the air had a large patch torn out of its trouser. "Fffff . . . fuckin' sssssssnake."

There was a stir among the bent backs. "Watch it!" someone screamed.

"Shit, it's alive." The men in the center began to yell and jump. "Stomp it. Stomp it good." They leaped up, boots flailing, heels in the air, spinning, clicking, bicycle-pedaling, coming down hard with a stamp.

"Yeeeeeeeh haw! Ride 'em. Riiiide 'em, cowboy."

"Hide out, here ah come. Ah'm out to chaw."

"Cock a doodle dooooh!"

"Ah'm spoilin'."

Hooting, shouting encouragement to one another, throwing their caps up, they danced.

"Salt me down."

"Roar and squeal. This meat is goin' bad."

"Bust it in. Stomp 'er down. Whoooh hah!"

The midget pranced in their midst, throwing his ten-gallon Stetson up, catching it, jingling the spurs on his boots, kicking. O'Dougherty heard a sickened cry above the din, but it was drowned out by the tread of boots as the men whistled, blew kisses at each other, their eyes moist.

"I'm a little Cupid!"

"Hug me! Ah'm a grizzly bayuh," as they danced on their heels, jabbing, jeering.

Between the flashing bowstrings of pants legs, black and brown hammer of shoes and boots, he saw a small battered body, a shred of tongue, broken nose, bits of ear clinging to the bashed skull, cheeks and eyes dug out. Detached from the bleeding neck, a clerical collar rolled in a pool of gore, back and forth like a circus hoop.

"Dddddd . . . dohsee Doh! Ssssss . . . swing your partner. Nnnnnn . . . now back to back." The Continentals clapped, swung each other, caught the nearest hand, and whirled around in a crude square dancing, lifting their spattered trousers. The midget screeched the steps.

"All join in," they chorused, snatching at members of the crowd. Everyone tried to get into the circle. One grabbed O'Dougherty's arm, yanking him toward the Bacchanalia. Dora was pulled along.

"Come on, have some fun!" O'Dougherty stared into the face of the TV announcer. The circle was coming apart, people linking in couples. Dora was broken out of his grasp, her fingers in flame, dragged away. The force of it staggered O'Dougherty. He lurched to the side, saw her in tow with the midget, her skirt hiked around her thighs, the panties at her knees, men shrieking, whistling, reaching out to get a finger on. Kissed, bitten, floating naked among them, she was screaming and laughing.

His own pants had come down about his ankles and as he stooped to pull them up and push after her, a blow knocked him off his feet. The crowd closed over his head in a flood.

He was kicked, shoved, squeezed through depths of arms, legs, fingernails, shoes, knees, struck at him. In a tidal roll, he was hurled, going black, coming to, dashed back into darkness again as the seas of bodies surged, tumbled, tossed higher, higher, rose roaring in the corridors, masses of panic. He gasped for air, digging at crotches, joints, battered into rear ends, plummeting down, smacking the concrete of the floor, then propelled up, in an ebb or backflow, almost seeing light he clutched at shoulders, chins, noses, anything to pull himself out of the mackerel press, slide, scraped along the side of a wall, the blood drumming in his nostrils as his forehead bowled along, bone-chipping. A corner held him for a moment; he sucked in air, then the rush, velocity, wedged him out, passed. . . .

Into the deeps he shot, awkward, half-mammal, half-fish. The sea was full of mirror horrors, golden-haired boys with long white penises and woman's breasts, swimming in the subterranean drift; human heads joined to the jelly of octopus flesh, sharks with hairy vaginas and lovely, tapering legs, a whale thrashing the waters with elephantine testicles; and hundreds of others wiggling from the growth of black, fetid seaweed, darting in and out of its slime.

A school of creatures like to himself, a huge number stretching beyond sight, streaked by. He could not see them singly, breasts, hair, bones, but as one undulating white patch. And he could not help himself but was drawn to them, swimming, sucked into the school, naked, writhing, wriggling, felt the oily bodies of his tribe rubbing, rippling, exciting him, as he mounted the gleaming scales of the buttocks before him, felt behind him a burst of sudden, delicious heat, and then glowing, ecstatic, the whole ocean dissolved in glowing pearly white, he tasted beads of flowing, dripping nectar, sweetness of white, white

"Fuuuuuuuuuuuuuuck!" cried the whole Colosseum. Blinking, O'Dougherty saw sun spots in front of him, the fierce floodlights sweeping through the vast circle, he could hardly look, the bowl of black uniforms turning dizzily. He was in the midst of it, a breaker of the crowd had flung him there, through the doorway of a ramp, into a group that was jammed between the seats in the aisle. He craned his neck, breathing deeply, trying to get a view over the heads around him.

Grease was pouring off the walls and columns of the stadium like sweat. It ran with the smell of old cotton candy, smudged chocolate, stale popcorn, beer, piss, cheap wine, armpits; spread through the seats, over the crowd, fuel to the pandemonium that O'Dougherty saw everywhere.

The banners of the Massachusetts delegation were before him. Fists swung among the heads, empty beer cans. A man next to O'Dougherty caught one in the eye. "Mother Machree," "Molly Malone," "My Wild Irish Rose," the Irish contingent's singing was loudest and drowned out the rest as they poured rye and Scotch on each other's suits and slugged the bottles back and forth. Swaying, he thought he recognized the face of one of his father's old campaign workers, crooning with shut eyes. Cheeks glistening with tears of Jack Daniel's, his uniform soaked in beer, a nose bulbous, ruby, bruised black and blue, bleeding from a cut above his puffed eye, the drunk mumbled, "Burn the goddamn place. . . ." The shoulders tight about held the rummy up. He spit into their faces.

"Handsome Dan!" one of them called, pinching the skinny wreck's cheeks so hard, he lashed out with his bottle. It broke in the face of a man. O'Dougherty saw a mat of flesh laced with crimson turning toward him. He screamed. A lighted match was thrown at the drunk. It caught in his white hair, which began to flame. "When Johnny comes marchin' home again, Haroom! Haroom!" A chorus about the fire, John O'Dougherty was in its midst. O God, he swore it. A cock flapped its wings above him, crowing, in wild accompaniment to the song.

The Rhode Island troops next to Massachusetts had brought several dozen prize fowl. Above Massachusetts, Vermont had stalled three or four cows.

There were mascots everywhere. A moose was tethered with chains to a pole. It stamped its hooves and butted with a powerful spread of antler, disdaining the bale of hay. The beast, its Brobdingnagian muscle clumping, chafed, gathering fury in the heat, jostling of the convention.

The explosions that rocked the walls, the shouts, fist fights, were upsetting animals throughout the stands. In Alabama donkeys switched their tails, jumping away from the hands trying to calm them. The drove of large possums penned in among the Arkansas limits milled furiously squeaking. Half-crazy with their smell, across the aisle in Mississippi, bloodhounds bayed; while shotguns, pistols, cans were being discharged into the air, Arkansas trying to beat off the oversized bald eagle that had slipped out of its strap in Washington, D.C., and was circling above. The bird ranged in a wider arc, bringing it over a herd of 12 Texas longhorn. The steers turned with lowered heads, their sharp horns pricking, blood dripping from their sides, eyes watering. The Texans were harassing these pets, lassoing, tying them up, burning tattoos into the animals' sides with cigar butts. One bellowing steer was dragged off from the herd and attacked with penknives, jammed down between the seats, trussed, a couple of overweight Austin cowboys sat on it while chunks of meat were cut from its shanks and belly. The steaks were broiled under the dying animal's nose. "Home, home on the range," howled three or four Houston oilmen as they poured whiskey into its wounds.

Overhead the eagle flapped its wings, ready to swoop, one eye on the Lone Star feast, the other fixed on Montana. Four mountain rams set to butting each other in the aisle. A female was bound, close enough for them to smell. One of the men had mounted the female from behind, "Git her sex glands goin'!" he cried, diddling. The scent of heat was grease on the backs of the chairs. Rams rushed at angles, turned in circles, banging horns on the steps. Idaho's cougar snarled, clawing at the concrete floor, crouching, jumping, pulled back in midair by its collar.

And above all, at the top of the stadium, the paws of Gargantua, hairy with silver-tipped fur, *Ursus horribilis,* a thousand pounds of grizzly seething at the slats.

A fire had started in the Massachusetts seats. It spread quickly through the carpet of trash underfoot, feeding on chocolate bars, chewing-gum wrappers, cigarette boxes, Dixie cups, containers, bunting, papier mâché, socks, shoes, pants legs. The flames rose among the cows in New Hampshire, which bawled, blinded by smoke.

High in the Maine delegation, the moose sniffed the air. Lifting antlers broad as a car, bone ivory, it reared, calling out in a low, clear bugle that echoed through the Colosseum. Settling to the floor, it rolled, twisting the chain around its body, then reared again, snapping the steel links, and as the fire touched its hooves, the great animal sprang into the air, soaring over the heads of New England, a covey of hens flapping behind.

Maine scrambled through the brush fire with sooty faces to recapture the mascot. The moose had bolted through Connecticut, New York, New Jersey and Maryland. Mississippi's hounds rushed forward to meet it.

The brown shadow kicked them lifeless over the seats. Enraged, Mississippi began firing.

"Chicken fuckers!" shouted the Maine men. Taking up their own guns, they began picking off Mississippi dogs. Alabama, Georgia, Florida, Carolina fired back. Caught in a volley among the Virginia seats, Maine sent back for reinforcements.

The moose had galloped into Texas, with a flick of its head caught an Austin dude, thrown him in the air. The steers, seeing the rush of their unspayed cousin, broke, followed, razorous. The dude came down on a rank of hooked bayonets, went under the charging steers. Down came the eagle among them and rose in a flapping of wings, its snow-white head feathers running vermilion, a fat buttock in its talons.

Rubber truncheons, six shooters, a grenade going off. Maine had been pushed back to Pennsylvania. The troops that should have been scrambling to their aid were battling. Three posts from Harlem had attacked an upstate lodge with razors. New York City was in an uproar, East Siders hurling Molotov cocktails at Queens, Staten Island, Riverdale.

Yet Illinois, Wisconsin, Iowa, the Midwest was pressing down on the Southern flank. The maimed Texans, gored, limping, tried to hold the line. Arkansas played dead with its possums, tongues out, limbs rigid, lying in urine.

The moose rocketed back over them and wheeling, Westward ho! Sprinting, driving the bighorns before it, breasted the leash of the cougar, set the cat aflight.

The bear, shuffling in its cage, faster and faster, throwing its half ton of weight against the side—the moose, big horns, hit the enclosure head on, tumbling it over and, with the grizzly inside, it began to roll down over the seats into Idaho, Wyoming, Colorado; the *Ursus horribilis* growling, biting, tearing as the slats shattered, chains severed. It made its escape in Arizona.

Hardly noticed, the Southwest was beset by a Mexican-American revolt. Riots were breaking out in LA. The bear shambled toward an exit through confusion; fires, shooting, charging animals, in which old wounds were reopened. Milwaukee's Germans tried to exterminate a Bronx detachment of Jews. Poles were massing in Illinois preparing to wipe out the Irish. Rhode Island's Italians had driven the Yankee and Celtic contingent out of state. A band of Indians was busy scalping among South Dakota. Religious differences kept reshaping the lines, Catholics against

Protestants, Episcopalians against Unitarians, Baptists vs. Seventh Day Adventists, Quakers against the field.

Into the bowl of fire, shouting, shooting, beating, ran a goon squad trying to extinguish the flames. A corps of ex convicts, Chicago Cops, Ku Kluxers, Black Panthers, Nazis, Teamsters, Mafiosi, Green Berets, Youth against War and Fascism, with spiked clubs, razors in their shoes, lead pipes, pistols, machine guns. They set up a mortar.

The moose, reaching the top of the stadium, facing the blank wall, wheeled. They were lobbing shells, trying to hit it. Pulling back, it arched against the sheer concrete face, then dashed so fast, hardly visible, a blur, it left the seats, soared into the air, stretching its proud head of horn.

The sight stopped the fighting.

Bugling, bugling, it crashed—breaking its neck on the stadium floor.

And at that moment a brace of trumpets blew over the loudspeaker system.

Drums were rolling. The bands which had been cowering on the rim of the arena, formed ranks and began to march forward. Bunched together, the musicians blared and banged as hard as they could on their instruments. In the wide-open space of the Colosseum's floor they were perfect targets. The crowd, waiting for three hours for the night to start, was going to let it out on someone. Only, behind them, just as the missiles began to fall . . .

The main doors of the arena, under the bandstand, were thrown open. A huge float moved out slowly, under the lights. The truck was draped in red with banks of scarlet and white carnations making crosses on the side. A figure seated on a tall throne topped the floral pyramid. It extended a rigid, fatherly hand in blessing through the rich, sanguine robes of the Church.

O'Dougherty heard the voice of the TV announcer crack the loudspeaker.

". . . as His Eminence passes before you, we ask you all, whatever denomination, to observe a respectful silence for this great prince, one of our earliest supporters. We would like to thank the Boston diocese at this time for loaning us the body of the cardinal. Let us receive his silent blessing." And in the amazed hush that pervaded the seats, the float bearing the cardinal rolling around the arena after the band, three men stepped from the open doors of the band room and in time to the funereal drum beat, marched out.

"Ladies and gentlemen, the Commander!"

Out of the foot stomping, huzzaing, wild ovation; confetti, caps, cans, bottles, ashtrays; the applause crashing down, "Kill me! Kill me!" they were screaming, baring their chests, the three emerged at the foot of the platform in the midst of the floor.

They climbed the steps. A huge pole rose through the center of the platform and continued up almost to the ceiling like a mast. The Commander began to climb this spar while the Reverend Billy Jim put up his hand for quiet.

"You got the blessing, here comes the invocation."

A claw struck the air.

" 'O harlot, hear the word!

" 'Because your filthiness was poured out, your nakedness uncovered.' That's Ezekiel talking, boys. He don't mince no words. He don't shit around the bush. Who's he talkin' 'bout? 'I will gather them against thee, from every side to see thy nakedness.' Who? 'They're gonna strip thee of thy clothes, thy fair jewels, leave thee naked and bare, gonna look at your tits, your ass, your cunt, gonna stone you with stones and thrust you with swords. A horror and spoil.' Who? Who? Who is it? Who is that gal?"

The reverend's face began to work now, the veins throbbing in his forehead as he lashed out the answer, "My country!"

"Ain't she pretty? Mmmmmmm . . ." he hummed, salacious, through the microphone, "Mmmmmmmm. . . ."

"She's been buggered and fucked. Mother fuckin'. Father fuckin'. Sister fuckin' and brother fuckin'. She's *opened her legs to all that passed.* She's neighed like a horse. She's showed her private parts to one and all.

"As the prophet says, 'She's been *payin* 'em to come and give it to her.

" 'She's painted herself, decked herself, lay back in bed, let them pour that lust out and pollute her.

" 'Gather round, she's got a cup to drink. Deep and large, full of drunkenness and sorrow. Drink it, drain it, crunch the shards thereof. Tear your breasts, whore, tear!' "

Billy Jim called out, "There's a parable. I git to quote," he hooted.

Set on the pot, set it on,
Pour in the water,
Throw in the thigh bone
And the shoulder,
Boil well,
Seethe, seeeeeethe.

" 'Woe to the bloody city, to the pot whose filth is therein, whose filth has not gone out. Heap on the wood. Kindle the fire. That the flesh may be consumed. Set it empty on the coals. Let the bottom burn. Let the shit be molten in it.' "

The preacher beat the air with his arms. "It ain't gittin' no better. It's got to be purged. She's filthy yet.

"What's that mean? It means fire and the sword. Before Peace there is War. This land is polluted. It's a lewdness. An abomination. A whore!

"It's written!" he screamed, jabbing elbows into his side.

A sword, a sword! It is sharpened,
Furbished,
Sharpened to make a sore slaughter,
Furbished to glitter,
The sword it is sharpened,
It's furbished,
To give into the hand of the slayer.

"Who'm I talkin' 'bout?" he screeched into the microphone. "Who? Who?"

"Who's gonna handle that sword? Who? Who?"

"Who's gonna lead us? Who? Who?"

The crowd took up the cry, delirious. "Who? Who?" They stood up, making the stadium shake. "Who? Who?" Steadily, hypnotically, together, as loud as they could, "Who? Who?"

The slain shall be cast out,
The stench of carcasses shall come up,
The mountains shall be melted with blood
One more time!

"Who!" they roared. "Who!"

High above the floor, batteries of lights were blinding him. He could feel the slight motion of the spar he stood atop, swaying, come up between his legs.

The floods rolled around him, stars, constellations, the Milky Way, he caught himself at the edge.

"My country," he sang, in the low, thrilling voice that sent a shiver through O'Dougherty as he stood in the audience, the quivering animal body of which he was part.

"My country," he answered, irresistibly, with the crowd, drawling, moaning the words, the sound of them tearing in his breast, so that he felt that awful warmth spreading through him. He was ready to go, he knew not where, the brilliant light washing out lines, uniforms, height, depth, distinction of audience, stands, pole, swaying

"Is me. . . ."

Down into a black abyss, millions, motes, dust, echoed. O Lucifer. He could not keep his place on the masthead, not when they stretched toward the horror, joy, engulfing, melting, the heat. Star of the day.

"Sweet land . . ." O'Dougherty ripped at his shirt, the madness burning in his eye sockets, he saw nothing but fire, echoing the word, tumbling forward, all of them following the body in flight into the abyss. The ground of the Colosseum giving way. All of them falling, screaming into the hole, the hole, "Liberty! Liberty! Liberty! Liberty!"

His head banged, the trumpets that blew brought him back to consciousness. He was high at the top of the stadium. The Continentals were packed around him in one unbroken mass. A drill team was finishing its routine on the floor of the stadium. Restless, bored, the stands paid no attention, shifting, angry.

Nothing had happened yet. A dream through which he was shaken and bruised. The trumpets blew again. He put his hand to his head. Something was about to happen.

And yes, under the bandstand, the main doors of the arena floor, which he had seen before, now, in truth, it seemed, slowly, agonizingly, in their progress, were pushed, inch by inch, open. And out . . .

Some mysteries are best not solved. Take the deaths, for an instance, of Hitler and Christ, to mix outrageously a saint and an evil madman. Our imagination, our sense of religious, divine significance, resists their abrupt passage into death, the unknown, the meaningless, the insignificant. We cannot believe the story ends at the crucifixion or the flames by the bunker. One escapes to Heaven, the other to Argentina. And setting aside the role in this of the Divine, you must admit that the popular imagination, quite apart from sacred texts, has woven its colorful threads on after they have been officially snapped, not wanting to surrender Frankensteins or Robin Hoods to a last, final tale. Always waiting for the thrill, the chill of their return.

So, too, I am loath to tell the end.

Indeed, the end is not clear.

One can report with a fair certainty some resolutions. We know, for example, that according to the coroner's report, the Reverend Billy Jim Jones was killed almost at the instant of impact by a .45 caliber bullet which entered the cerebrum, shattering skull fragments through the midbrain. The bullet could not be identified positively as coming from the gun found in possession of Paul Gogarty (who is listed as having died in shock from massive blood loss in an ambulance carrying him to the same New Jersey hospital where the body of Billy Jim was autopsied), because said bullet, despite an extraordinarily careful and detailed search by members of the Jersey City Police assisted by agents of the Federal Bureau of Investigation and other interested government agencies, could not be found. We are faced with only a probability.

Both bodies are presumed to be lying under their respective markers: one below an ostentatious column of black New Hampshire granite towering high over the crowded neighboring stones in the Catholic cemetery at the edge of Boston called New Calvary; the other rests humbly, marked by a simple wooden white cross in the humid soil of a tiny roadside plot by the dirt track of an Alabama village.

The pomp and circumstance of the first funeral, the figure, decently covered, which lay at full view in the lobby of City Hall for two days while friends and dignitaries of the Commonwealth filed by to assure themselves that the corpse smiling up at them was indeed himself: all this makes me relatively secure in alleging that the body is pinned under that granite. Many who viewed the cadaver reported that it was so lifelike that the dead face was even sweating through the makeup.

Although the second interment was marked by no crowds, the plot has not been neglected. Several of the neighboring organizations have made it the site of their secret oaths and pledges. Weekly in cap and gown they meet at midnight, as if the body's presence would hover over their activities.

Ark, the Hollywood movie idol, simply disappeared from sight. Whether he was wounded, killed, a victim of foul play, nobody knows, or at least no one who does will talk about it.

As for William Star, although his death was reported in the papers, making banner headlines, there is no coroner's report to be found, no mention of a final resting place, no determination of the cause of his demise.

The story of Star's life, of course, out of regard for all and respect for the dead, was buried. Like so many others, it is known to a few hardened reporters, part of their cynical equipage.

Ah, but I have rushed ahead in my hasty way. Let us return to events: the moment when Ark, wounded, pushed open the huge doors into the stadium.

The actor staggered a few feet forward into the arena. As the portals swung out, trumpets had announced the final, momentous event of the Convention. Their call had hushed the men and hullabaloo. Every face looked to the parting gates. From every point in the bowl, the great batteries of lights shot toward a pinpoint of focus, thousands and thousands of floods shattered their beams in the small circle, millions of watts blazed in the cone of brilliance that blasted at the center of the doors in the spot where Ark, slumping, collapsed.

His body burned under the immense candlepower.

It lay there. No one moved. Was it a joke? There had been so many tricks at the gatherings preceding this that the packed hall remained obediently silent. Only after a long, long stillness did people begin to stir in their seats. One or two in each delegation would lean across the aisle to ask if the neighboring state knew what was going on. At first they were shushed, and had to sit back in their chairs to disapproving looks. It was after 15 or 20 minutes that the ranks began to cough and grunt. Their officers tried to shut them up, but here and there someone would mutter that there was something wrong. At last, an impatient little man in one of the delegations got up and began to walk down the aisle.

No one stopped him. The Continentals watched as he clattered down the long series of steps from the top of the bowl to the ring around the arena. Looking about, he paused, then jumped over the guard rail and started to walk toward the body. The assemblage expected that the goon squad would grab him, throw him back; and he too, for he stopped a few yards from the rail to see if they were after him. But they were staring at him with the rest of the convention.

He resumed his steps, reached the body, bent down and then, looking into the open band room, squinting in the glare, he started running toward it. Now dozens, hundreds were getting up and going down the aisles. They clambered over the barrier and came toward the body. A crowd milled around Ark as the entire convention rose in the stadium and began to descend to the floor to see what had happened.

Yet there was hardly a sound, except for the shuffling of their feet. The talk had died away. No one asked anymore what had happened. They simply pushed forward to get a look at what was lying on the bottom of the arena. As the crowding around it grew more and more, those who had seen it not moving away but just standing, looking at the ground, a silent struggle broke out, tight-lipped men behind quietly shoving as hard as they could.

The doors of the band room had been shut. Those who had first seen the figure on the floor were pressed back against the metal doors and squeezed up against them, crushed.

"Cccccc . . . come on, you ccccc . . . cock sssssssuckers. Cccccc . . . cut it out!" a voice squeaked over the loudspeakers. "Gggggg . . . give it air. Air! Aaaaaaaa . . . air!"

At this, roused by the sudden command, the goon squad began to collect together and, stuporous, moved into the crowd, lifting their sticks, swinging the billies back and forth as if half-asleep.

"Cccccc . . . come on. Bbbbbbbb . . . back! Bbbbbbbb . . . back!"

The men did not resist but, directed by the clubs, cleared back, leaving a space around the body. The house doctor now came out, escorted by the squad, and stooped over it. The doors of the band room opened again, a crack, and it was brought in. The gates shut behind it.

"Nnnnnnn . . . nothing has hhhhhhhh . . . happened."

A few minutes later, as the men were being shepherded away from the doors, the speakers announced, "Jjjjjj . . . just an accident."

The crowd stood, half in the stands, half in the arena, listening as at short intervals from the public-address system, the facts were detailed. A series of bulletins were stuttered out.

The convention, in a state of shock, learned that a gun had gone off. Ricocheting bullets had nicked some of their leaders. If everyone would remain calm, the business of the evening would soon resume. A doctor was seeing to them now.

Soon after this, they heard that the injuries had become more serious. Complications set in. "Ssssss . . . stand by for ffffff . . . further developments."

The troops gathered close to one another, huddling, noiseless, at attention in what seemed to last forever, for a scratchy, high squawk.

"Vvvvvvv . . . Vice Commander GGGGGGGGG . . . Gogarty is dddddd . . . dead."

A sigh, a sound of sadness yet relief, passed through the men bunched together. It echoed under the ceiling like the low note of an accordion. They waited for the band to play appropriate music, a funeral march; or a prayer to start. Only, these did not come.

"VVVVVV . . . Vice Commander JJJJJJ . . . Jones is ddddddd . . . dead."

The ranks stiffened. One by one the lamps in the bowl were being extinguished. The shadow of the central pole fell across the seats as the suns of the ceiling waned. The arena was shrouded in darkness. Only the emergency and the exit lights glowed.

"CCCCCCC . . . Commander Star is dddddd . . ."

Contrary to what might have been expected, there was no panic. The crowd, asked to leave, prodded by marshals, began to back toward the exits, slowly, heads lowered, with suspicious looks. In knots, mumbling among themselves, they filed through the corridors, past the wreckage of the night.

Costumes torn, haggard, the ache of a long hangover breaking between their eyes, they stumbled among the broken chairs, cans, paper. The floors were wet. The plumbing had been ripped out.

Above their bare pates, the first rib of dawn was piercing the sky. It was cold outside. They hunched their shoulders and crept toward cars and bus stops. They would drive all day and night, back to Dubuque, Albuquerque, San Luis Obispo, decent, sane folks, to sleep.

Through the plastic bubble over the circle of trash, the body of morning casts its gray, early pall. There was still no illumination in the corridors. And no searching ray had yet broken the pitch black of a locked ladies' room in the basement where Dora, nude, was propped over a toilet bowl, her face floating under the water, drowned. Nor could the last, departing attendants see the form of the man on his knees, kneeling at the bottom of a ramp in the corner, telling a string of rosary beads over and over. O'Dougherty locked in his penitence. The dossier missing. They heard him but did not stop to take him out. He is ignored.

As is the telephone ringing in an empty apartment.

Meanwhile, a ship, a freighter was slowly, awkwardly turning its great bulk, shearing the Hudson waters as it executed in mid-river a turn of 360 degrees. The black currents pour from its aft parts, a rusty sewer flood in its wake.

Iron, it rusts from bow to stern, no paint sticks to the sides. A cold wind precedes it down the river.

In the hold, rats are shivering with the plague. They huddle together for the warmth of the fever.

It is an old ship. The keel is wood, unscraped for centuries. Four hundred years ago, perhaps it sailed with nothing but grape and cannon ball, a few casks of powder and a secret. Its terror, silent, spreading on the wings of mosquitoes, the scrambling of mice along the deer paths, leaving behind tents, campfires, and rotting corpses. The ghosts of Indian villages across the continent.

Now, heavily laden, it rides low on the waves out to sea. Its bows are piled high with boxes. Unopened crates of chemicals, test tubes. The stuff of ingenious chemists, biologists; stoppered blights, rots, vials of pox and murrain, old, new. Gases of all description, carelessly packed, the means to multiply all noisome things upon the land, gnats, locusts, beetles. Also the formulae of physicists, most fearful, so, as it is prophesied, the earth may truly "totter and tremble, reel to and fro like a drunken man . . . break, break down, crumble in pieces. . . ."

No officers, no deckhands, except the animals locked below. A pig is playing with the helm. A vulture stares from the lookout.

It drifts for other shores, other opportunities, that ancient, floating box of ills.

A bottle is flung from the deck and bobs toward shore. Inside a note:

COME! HEAR!

You are invited to attend timely,
spiritually strengthening talks.

April 9
Where are the dead?

April 18
A Son Loyal—
And those who Rebelled

April 27
Holiness Rules
Soon a Paradise Earth

ALL TALKS 9:00 P.M.

Holiness Hall
999 Avenue D
(3rd Floor)
New York, N.Y.

ALL INTERESTED PERSONS WELCOME

FREE FREE

NO COLLECTION